'I'm here because my boss sent me,' stated Naomi.

'It doesn't make sense for Davenport to select his best physician for a stint at our hospital. He hasn't in the past,' Adam replied.

'Maybe he wants to foster a good relationship between our facilities.'

'If that was truly his objective he'd assign someone who wants to be in Deer Creek,' Adam said. 'Not an individual who's only putting in time until he or *she*—' he glared at her '—can move on to bigger and better things.'

Naomi shrugged. 'Until the person you want appears on your doorstep you'll have to settle for me. Now, if you don't mind, Doctor,' she said in a dismissive tone, 'I have work to do.'

Dear Reader

I'm delighted to introduce you to Bethany, Kirsten and Naomi in the *Sisters at Heart* trilogy. I've always enjoyed reading books with a common thread and wanted to create one of my own. Someday.

When a close friend moved to another community, I knew that 'someday' had arrived. While bemoaning the lost opportunities for spur-of-the-moment walks and the lack of a readily available sympathetic ear, I couldn't help but reminisce about my other close friends. I have a special place in my heart for those who accepted me into their circle when I, as a teenager, advanced from small country schools to one with nearly a thousand students. We laughed together and cried together, shared our dreams and aspirations, and weathered the storms on our way to adulthood.

Consequently, when I met Beth for the first time, I understood how important her friends were to her and saw how their early camaraderie shaped their lives, making them as emotionally close as sisters. They shared many experiences and interests, and from that this series came into being.

I invite you to meet three women whose friendship has withstood the test of time. I hope that you, too, have several friends who are your 'sisters at heart'.

Happy reading!

Jessica Matthews

TOO CLOSE
FOR COMFORT

BY
JESSICA MATTHEWS

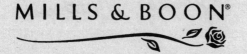

MILLS & BOON®

To Mary, for your insightful criticisms

*MILLS & BOON and MILLS & BOON with the Rose Device
are registered trademarks of the publisher.*

*First published in Great Britain 1997
Harlequin Mills & Boon Limited,
Eton House, 18-24 Paradise Road, Richmond, Surrey TW9 1SR*

© Jessica Matthews 1997

ISBN 0 263 80440 2

*Set in Times 10 on 12 pt. by
Rowland Phototypesetting Limited
Bury St Edmunds, Suffolk*

03-9711-44259-D

*Printed and bound in Great Britain
by Mackays of Chatham PLC, Chatham*

CHAPTER ONE

NAOMI STEWART wanted to go home.

Shielding her eyes against the bright June sun with duffel bag in hand, she paused on the sidewalk outside Deer Creek Hospital to stare at the structure before her. The three-story red brick building constructed in the 1940s was impressive for a town this size, but it didn't compare to her home turf. Lakeside Memorial in Kansas City boasted eighteen floors and countless offices on its fifteen-acre campus, and possessed state-of-the-art medical equipment in every field of medicine.

It was hard to say what instrumentation Deer Creek had—she'd only been here a few hours and most of that time had been spent in the emergency room. Even when her boss, Walter Davenport, had delivered his ultimatum last week he hadn't given many details and she'd been too stunned by the turn of events to ask.

She winced, remembering the week-old conversation and the cold feeling of despair which had encircled her. Having her name removed from the duty roster had been more painful than a surgical incision without anesthetic.

Granted, Walter couldn't have ignored her fainting spell in ER, but she'd hoped that it would have gone unnoticed. Unfortunately, interesting tidbits of gossip spread faster among the staff than a contagious disease and no amount of arguing on her part had convinced Davenport to rescind his ruling.

In the end, she had had two choices—either take a

leave of absence or choose the slower pace of Deer
Creek for three months until she'd totally recovered—
neither of which had thrilled her. Visibility was important to her promotion and working at a facility an hour's
drive southeast of Kansas City wouldn't provide the
same opportunities as working in Lakeside's busy ER.

By the same token, competition for the shift supervisor position was too fierce for her to spend time
lounging around her apartment.

So she'd chosen the lesser of the two evils and within
moments of her decision had found herself face to face
with a Deer Creek physician.

Less than a week later she'd been established in temporary accommodation with such ease that she couldn't
help but suspect that she'd been maneuvered into this
assignment.

Beads of perspiration lined her forehead and she
wiped them away. She took a bracing breath and
squared her shoulders, before making her way back to
the air-conditioned department she had left only minutes
earlier.

Heat radiated off the concrete walkway and she grate-
fully stepped through the automatic doors leading
directly into Emergency Services. Once inside she
couldn't help but make more comparisons.

Deer Creek had only one trauma room and three
individual exam cubicles as opposed to Lakeside's five
trauma rooms and seven individual cubicles. She was
accustomed to a waiting room with three dozen or more
chairs, filled to standing-room-only capacity at any
given point in time, not eight seats which also accom-
modated the patients waiting for their turn in Radiology.

The contrast between her familiar world and this foreign one glared at her.

Still, the occupants of those eight chairs had kept her busy—not by Lakeside's hectic standards, but busy nonetheless—until a few minutes ago when she'd stolen a few minutes to go to her car.

Lacey Olsen, the nurse-practitioner, waved her arms frantically in the distance and captured Naomi's attention. Naomi speeded her approach to the nurses' station just as Lacey replaced the microphone on the two-way radio unit.

'A Code Blue's coming in, Dr Stewart,' Lacey said.

Naomi dropped the black nylon bag she was carrying onto an empty chair. She'd retrieved her personal belongings in hopes of slipping off her best dress and into a more utilitarian scrub suit but, with this announcement, all such thoughts fled. 'Vital signs?'

'No pulse. Paramedics are giving CPR.' Lacey eyed Naomi's attire. 'If you want to change clothes you have two minutes.'

'I won't even try,' she said with a tired smile. 'Maybe when we're finished with this case I will.'

'The way the morning's been, I wouldn't count on it,' the honey-blonde nurse in her mid-twenties warned. 'Sorry we're running you ragged on your first day.'

Naomi shrugged. 'No problem.' Privately she scoffed at Walter Davenport's reassurances that this assignment would be relaxing and non-stressful. Before the ink had dried on her signature in the personnel office the human resources director had sent her to lend her assistance in the emergency room.

She'd expected to have a leisurely first day, learning hospital policy and procedures, but instead she'd been thrust into the action. She had yet to find the ladies' restroom, but she'd already seen ten patients and now a code blue was on its way.

Lacey, however, had been a godsend. The nurse was a fount of information and her obvious joy at Naomi's presence had gone a long way toward making Naomi feel less inadequate.

The wail of a distant siren was cut short, signaling the arrival of the ambulance. Naomi, Lacey and Tim, the graduate nurse with a football player physique, hurried toward the automatic doors, ready to receive their patient.

Two paramedics in light blue Fire Department uniforms rushed in, one pushing and the other guiding a gurney which carried a markedly obese man with heart monitor leads attached to his chest.

'Seventy-eight-year-old male. No pulse,' one reported as the group steered the victim into the trauma room. 'The monitor's been flat since we arrived on the scene. No history of heart disease. His wife reported he was fine one minute, then toppled out of his chair. She initiated CPR.'

'Time?' Naomi asked.

'About twenty minutes.' The thirtyish EMT with short, sandy-colored hair, who also appeared to be in charge, stopped his chest compressions and stepped aside.

Without a pulse and signs of heart activity, Naomi held no hope as she performed her examination. The lack of any spontaneous respiration, the fixed pupils and deep unconsciousness were unmistakable clinical signs.

She straightened, stripping off her gloves. 'That's it,

guys. Time of death. . .' she glanced at the wall clock '. . .oh-nine-ten.'

For a few seconds everyone froze, as if to pay their last respects. With the drama over, Naomi glanced at the light-haired senior paramedic directly across from her. The silver tag on the flap of his right breast pocket displayed his name—DALE SIMONSON—in black letters.

Dale wiped the sheen of sweat off his brow with his bare forearm. 'Chester Lang was a great guy. Had a feeling he was gone when we got there. . .'

'I'm sure he was,' Naomi agreed. The men's actions had been futile, but since CPR had been in progress only a physician could pronounce the man dead and discontinue the procedure.

Over the next few minutes the group worked in silence to disconnect the monitors and other equipment from Mr Lang's body. Once the EMTs had gathered their belongings Dale turned to Lacey and grinned. 'Hey, Lace. Coffee ready yet?'

Lacey rolled her eyes. 'Do I look like a waitress? Is getting a caffeine jolt the only thing on your mind?'

Dale laughed and a mischievous gleam appeared in his eyes. 'You're all I think about. How about a movie tonight?'

Lacey blushed, then whipped the privacy curtain around the body. 'I'm busy,' she said pertly. 'And, yes, the coffee's ready. Before you go this is our new ER doctor, Naomi Stewart. So be on your best behavior.'

Dale wore a look of mock outrage. 'We always are.' He glanced at Naomi, giving her a sincere smile. 'Nice meeting you. Good luck.'

'Thanks.'

He turned to his younger cohort. 'Come on, Rich. Let's get a cup of Java before someone drains the pot. Ladies, until next time.' With that parting statement, the two men left.

'You know, I don't think I've ever been told, "Good luck," as often as I have since I arrived here,' Naomi mused aloud. 'It's almost as if I'm going into battle.'

Lacey appeared uncomfortable. 'I suppose you are. Most of the staff don't think highly of the doctors Lakeside sends to staff our emergency room. In fact, there's talk about the merger falling through if we can't reach a mutual settlement on this particular issue.'

Davenport had made it clear that Lakeside's CEO would look favorably on anyone who navigated these choppy waters successfully. Obviously there were more undercurrents than she'd expected.

'We've had a lot of problems, especially with their attitudes. For some reason, they thought their job here would be easy.'

Davenport's comment about her time in Deer Creek being like a paid vacation echoed in Naomi's mind, and she avoided Lacey's gaze to studiously record her notes in Lang's chart.

Lacey glanced at the body and sighed. 'What a shame that Chester's time ran out today, of all days. Adam treated him for years and I don't recall there ever being a question of heart disease.'

Naomi raised her head. 'Do you mean Adam Parker?'

Lacey nodded.

A sickening feeling flooded over her as Naomi imagined his reaction. Walter Davenport had been close-mouthed about the situation in Deer Creek, but Parker's name had been mentioned as being dissatisfied with the quality of physicians Lakeside had supplied to staff the emergency room. Although Mr Lang's demise had been out of her control, she doubted if Dr Parker would see it that way.

Once again she sent forth a silent wish.

She wanted to go home.

'There's something you should know.'

Adam Parker shortened his stride to match Henry Alan Taylor's shorter steps. 'Sounds ominous. What's up?' he asked as they strode past a departing ambulance and onto the emergency room loading dock.

'Our new ER physician starts today.'

Adam stopped just inside the hallway to stare at the older man in disbelief. 'Today? Why didn't you tell me before now?'

'Because you've been on vacation for the past week. Remember?' Henry—or Hank, as he preferred to be called—dug in his pocket for a white handkerchief and wiped the sweat off his shaggy brow. 'It's hot for this time of morning, isn't it?'

Peering at Hank's ruddy face, Adam decided to send his partner and mentor home early for a much-deserved rest. Handling double duty was tough on anyone, and he had a thirty-year advantage over his sixty-eight-year-old colleague.

'Another scorcher in the making.' Adam steered the conversation back on the track he wanted. 'What's wrong with our new doctor?'

'Nothing.' Henry shook his sparsely covered gray head for emphasis.

His quick and hearty answer didn't relieve Adam's mind and he narrowed his eyes. 'Lakeside doesn't make

a habit of sending their cream-of-the-crop ER physicians to our facility. What's wrong with this one?'

Henry's grin was wide enough to reveal his silver
incisor. 'Don't you trust me?'

Adam ran one hand over his head, barely ruffling his
closely cropped hair. 'You I trust. Davenport's another
story, which is why I wanted you to talk to him. Being
an old friend of yours, he would listen to you.'

'He did. As it happens, he sympathized with us and
apologized.'

'Apologies aren't good enough. We need a physician
we can count on.'

'Which is why he's assigned his best doctor to us.'

Adam grimaced. 'He said that when he sent Bill
Carothers. Of course, he neglected to mention that Dr
Carothers was the best only when he was sober, which
wasn't very often.'

'Yes, well, apparently Bill was able to cover his
tracks before he came here. If we hadn't discovered
his problems he wouldn't be receiving treatment now,'
Hank said. 'Not only have we saved his patients, but
we may have saved a man's career.'

'I'm glad for him, but we can't be expected to screen
Lakeside's physicians. Deer Creek shouldn't be their
training ground.'

'I agree, but that isn't the case this time. I've read
Dr Stewart's file myself. It was filled with glowing
reports.'

Adam wrinkled his mouth. 'Dr Montgomery's file
said the same thing. Unfortunately, his brilliant mind
was more suited to research than actual clinical work—
a fact conveniently omitted.'

'You have to be open-minded,' Henry said, his voice stern.

Adam drew a deep breath. 'I suppose.' Thinking that the name rang a familiar bell, he thought a moment. 'I met a Ted Stewart at a seminar last fall. Seems to me he worked at Lakeside.'

Deciding that he was correct, he nodded. 'A decent fellow, too. At the time he wanted to move away from the big city.' He shrugged. 'If they sent him I can't complain.'

Henry screwed up his age-lined face as he rubbed one cheek in indecision. 'It isn't Ted.'

Adam stared at his partner. A few inches taller than his six-foot colleague, Adam had no trouble meeting his gaze. 'It isn't?'

'No. Her name is Naomi. Naomi Stewart.'

Adam crossed his arms over his comfortable green and black short-sleeved polo shirt. 'You've got to be joking,' he said, not bothering to hide his disgust. While he'd worked with a fair number of women physicians, the last two had soured his opinion of them. Both had complained of Deer Creek's relative isolation and both had left town before a year had passed.

Kandace's departure hadn't been surprising—she'd had no ties to bind her to the community and had made it perfectly clear that she wanted none.

Cynthia's parting of the ways, on the other hand, had been devastating. He'd lost not only a colleague and dreams of expanding his partnership but also a fiancée.

'I'm not. Dr Stewart comes highly recommended.'

'I'll bet.'

'Don't be so cynical or sarcastic. Naomi's being considered for a promotion. Shift supervisor.'

'All the more reason that she won't last. Dammit, Hank, we wanted a doctor who would stay, one willing to set down roots. The staff are tired of breaking in a new person every few weeks. From past experience we know that a single woman won't relocate here. We want a family man or a married woman, someone who wants to raise his or her kids in a wholesome environment.'

'Getting a doctor who knows their business is better than someone less qualified who is willing to live out the rest of his days in Deer Creek,' Hank pointed out. 'Wouldn't you agree?'

Adam shrugged in reply.

'Don't paint her with Cynthia's brush, or Kandace's either. Naomi is different.'

'That remains to be seen. Is it too much to ask Lakeside for a competent physician who wants small-town living? Who doesn't consider it a punishment to come here?'

Hank clapped his hand on Adam's shoulder. 'No, but until we find the right person we have to make allowances. Give Dr Stewart a chance.'

'Oh, I will,' Adam said, his voice grim. 'She'll get one and only one. The people of this community don't deserve to be treated like guinea pigs.'

'Adam.' Hank's tone was warning.

'Even if by chance she is "the best",' Adam continued, 'I can't believe Davenport would give her up in the interest of public relations. There's more behind his decision than meets the eye. She has a flaw of some sort and I intend to find it.'

'If you want to search out hidden motives, be my guest. I'm grateful to have daytime emergency room coverage again and, if you're as intelligent as I think you are, you should be grateful, too.'

'Oh, I am, although having Lakeside treat us like an unwanted stepchild is wearing on the nerves.'

'Merging is a difficult time for all of us,' Hank reassured him. 'Just be patient until the proverbial bugs get worked out. In the long run, we'll be better off being affiliated with Lakeside.'

'I hope you're right. Now, can we get on with this?' Adam's tone was resigned. 'I have sick people to see.'

'Hey, Lace,' Hank called out at the sight of the nurse, coming toward them with a paper in her hand. 'Has Dr Stewart arrived?'

'Two hours ago, and thank goodness,' she said cheerfully. 'We're haven't seen this many people at once in ages. Poor thing, she already looks worn to a frazzle.'

Adam frowned. 'She's here to pull her weight, not sit behind a desk and look pretty. If she can't handle the pace then she doesn't belong in ER.' Great, he thought to himself, tallying a point against her.

'I didn't say that,' Lacey corrected. 'It's tough falling into the thick of things before you've been properly oriented. I'd think you doctors would handle that aspect a little better than you do.'

Not in the mood for one of her famous tongue-lashings, he changed the subject. 'Where is she?'

Lacey pointed directly ahead. 'Trauma One. Shall I send her out?'

Realizing that only a few steps separated them, Adam inhaled a fortifying breath. 'No. We'll find her.'

'Suit yourself.' Lacey started toward the trauma room.

With Hank half a step ahead, Adam strode forward on soundless feet, impatient to perform his duty toward the new physician so that he could start his day. Having been gone for over a week, he had a lot of catching up to do and he refused to waste time welcoming someone he didn't want.

Inside the area designed to accommodate three injured patients at once Adam glanced at the unfamiliar toffee-haired woman who was standing in front of the pulled curtain, engrossed in a document. He couldn't tell much about her from his viewing angle.

Hank reached out, his voice hearty. 'Naomi. Welcome aboard.'

She looked up and Adam was momentarily taken aback by the sunny smile she bestowed on his colleague. She placed the clipboard in her hand on the counter and tucked a gold Cross pen into the left pocket of her white lab coat, before taking Hank's hand in hers.

'It's good to see you, Dr Taylor,' she answered.

'We cleared that up the other day—no more "Dr Taylor" stuff. It's Hank.'

She nodded, her bright blue eyes sparkling.

'I hear we've thrown you in at the deep end,' Hank said.

'It hasn't been so bad.'

Listening to her melodious voice from his place near Hank's elbow, Adam studied what he'd considered to be his latest headache with undisguised interest. Dr Stewart's face may have the classic girl-next-door appearance, with her high cheek-bones and too-wide mouth, but the rest of her didn't fit in that category.

Her long hair was braided, not just a simple braid but one of those elaborate styles that his sisters paid a small fortune for at the beauty shop.

The hospital-issue lab coat hung open and he saw

her dress—a silky affair with swirls of red, black and green on a white background—belted at her waist. Familiar with the designer-label clothing on which his sisters occasionally splurged, this garment fell in the same class. If she truly intended to be productive in ER she would have worn a practical scrub suit, not something that draped every willowy curve and was more suited for a Sunday tea.

Even the scent surrounding her was one he recognized from his recent shopping expedition for his mother's birthday gift. It was light and airy and horribly expensive.

All in all, it was apparent that her tastes leaned in the same extravagant direction as Cynthia's had— nothing but the best would suffice. He stiffened, gritting his teeth in the process. Naomi Stewart wouldn't survive at Deer Creek any more than Cynthia had.

To top it off, Dr Stewart also appeared young—much too young. He rubbed his chin. God, he must be getting old if medical schools were turning out physicians on the unsuspecting public who were barely adults.

'We don't want to scare you off on your first day.' Hank gestured to Adam. 'I'd like to introduce Adam Parker, my associate.'

For an instant her eyes widened. Then, with her face composed, she thrust out her right hand. 'Doctor.'

Her soft skin in his palm and her strong grip registered on Adam's mind as he focused on the brilliant blue of her irises—a color so intense that it had to result from contact lenses rather than genetics. In spite of the striking color, he saw something in her eyes—something that made her seem older than she appeared. Before he could define the exact characteristic Lacey whipped the cotton privacy curtain out of the way. The shrill sound of metal curtain rings rubbing against the curved metal rod caught his attention and he glanced in that direction without thinking.

He noticed a figure lying in the hospital bed—a figure covered from a head to toe with a sheet.

His doubts about Lakeside's so-called 'best' physician rose like a cloud of volcanic ash, and his welcoming arm dropped as if he'd been scalded.

Lakeside's 'best' had barely arrived and already someone had suffered the consequences with his life.

The mesmerizing spell of Adam's commanding presence and masculine vitality broke and a familiar taste of rejection filled Naomi's mouth. She shoved her hand into her lab coat pocket and fingered the shiny fifty-cent piece she carried to entertain uncooperative children.

From the time she'd overheard the question, 'What's wrong with him?' coming around the corner, she'd prepared herself to explain the circumstances of her patient's demise.

As time had gone on no one had appeared, and the tenor voice had faded until she could only pick up an occasional word. Her name, uttered in an unflattering tone, echoed once into the trauma room, alerting her that she was the topic of someone's conversation. To be specific, Adam Parker's conversation.

Naomi stiffened her spine under the full heat of his attention. Adam's stunned disbelief gave way to a set jaw and a tic appeared in his left cheek before he brushed past to uncover Lang's face.

Hank peered at the body. 'Heart attack?'

Naomi trained her gaze on the younger, taller and

more fit physician of Hank's partnership. 'Yes,' she said, revising her flawed mental image of Adam Parker. After meeting the elderly Hank and learning of their partnership, she'd pictured Adam as close to retirement age, always wearing a crisp professional suit and tie in keeping with his set ways and opinions. She'd never dreamed he'd be so close to her own age of thirty— although he was at least eight years older—and wearing casual hunter-green chino trousers with a matching open-necked polo shirt.

It wouldn't matter what he wore, she decided. Adam Parker exuded authority naturally; the clothes didn't matter. Yet, if he ever dressed for a formal occasion, he'd stand out like a prince among peasants.

If only some of Hank's charm had rubbed off on Adam. The older man's easy manner had relieved most of her concerns about working in Deer Creek, but since encountering Adam's hostility firsthand her doubts magnified tenfold.

The idea of being Lakeside's ambassador to this troubled little hospital seemed daunting and completely beyond her scope, but if she failed her career path at the larger hospital would come to a quick dead end.

Looking at the bright side, perhaps Parker's gruff behavior and outspoken ways were fortuitous. With a personality such as his, she'd never succumb to the initial sparks of attraction she'd felt.

'Chester never would slow down.' Hank shook his head. 'What a shame.'

'Yeah. Isn't it?' Adam's gaze never left Naomi's as he ran his hand over his ash blond hair, cropped short like a new recruit at boot camp. The few seconds of silence seemed like hours until Tim strode in, oblivious to the undercurrents flowing through the room.

'Need some help, Lace?' he asked.

'Sure,' she said, looking to Naomi for confirmation.

Naomi gave a brisk nod and a reassuring smile. Although she didn't doubt that she'd have to defend herself, she'd rather have fewer witnesses.

'By the way, Dr Taylor,' Tim added, 'Dr Lawrence in Radiology is looking for you.'

'Did he say what he wanted?'

'Something about some X-rays.'

'Probably the Ryan boy's sinus films. I'll stop by on my way out.' Hank appeared unconcerned.

'He seemed rather anxious,' Tim added.

As if aware of the potentially volatile situation between the two younger physicians, Hank frowned. 'Then I'd better see what's on his mind. I'll be right back.' After throwing Adam a warning glance, he left ahead of the two nurses on their way to the morgue.

Naomi retrieved the clipboard and her pen, intending to finish her paperwork.

Adam's voice broke the ensuing silence like a gunshot on a quiet evening. 'I saw Chester Lang a week ago. He was perfectly fine.'

She signed the death certificate. 'That sometimes happens with coronaries.'

'Did you try—?'

'We did everything possible,' Naomi said through gritted teeth. She laid the records on the counter none too gently. 'It's all here. Read it.'

His stance was rigid. 'Oh, I will, Miss Stewart, or do you prefer Ms?'

'Doctor will do just fine.'

A wry twist appeared on his mouth. 'I stand

corrected.' He pointedly checked his watch. 'What time did you come on duty?'

His quiet tone was as unexpected as the question itself. 'Eight o'clock. Seven fifty-five, to be exact. Why?'

'Less than two hours. You're to be congratulated.'

Puzzled, she asked, 'What for?'

'You've broken the record.'

'What record?'

'Dr Carothers lost his first patient on his second day of work. Dr Montgomery lost a woman at the end of his first shift. You, Dr Stewart, have beaten all of them.'

Naomi stared at him in mute horror until she found her voice. 'I resent that.'

'I'm only stating the obvious.'

'Situations aren't always what they seem.'

'Then enlighten me.'

She slowly folded her arms, maintaining eye contact. If he thought he could intimidate her by looking down his straight nose from his lofty height of well over six feet with his dark eyebrows drawn into a line then he could think again. His Adonis-like features might turn most women into mush, and a piercing gaze from his nut-brown eyes might make a lesser individual quake in his proverbial boots, but not her.

For a brief second she considered explaining how Mr Lang had been DOA—dead on arrival. Although she and her staff had gone through the motions of resuscitation, she knew, and so did the paramedics who had brought the patient in, that he'd died instantly at his home—not at the hospital.

Maybe if Adam hadn't already assumed the worst

she would have gone into detail, but he had and now her pride wouldn't let her.

'No.' She used an emphatic tone.

Adam looked taken aback, as if he'd never heard the two-letter word before. Then again, maybe he hadn't in recent years. 'No?'

'No. Your mind is already made up so I won't waste my time trying to convince you otherwise. Think whatever you like.'

His lips twitched. 'Are you always this vocal, Dr Stewart?'

'Only if the occasion demands it.'

He leaned against the counter and crossed his arms. 'Has Hank outlined your duties?'

Coolness replaced his former hostility and she didn't know which attitude posed more danger. Even so, she was glad for the change in subject. 'I cover ER during your peak times—six a.m. to six p.m. After that, the local doctors back up the nurse practitioners and physician assistants on an on-call basis for anything beyond their expertise.'

He nodded, as if the information was accurate. 'I understand you're being considered for a promotion.'

She shrugged. 'I've applied for a supervisory position and, yes, it would be a promotion.'

'Then why didn't Davenport keep you at Lakeside?'

CHAPTER TWO

'ARE you always this blunt?' Naomi asked, rephrasing the question Adam had posed to her a few minutes ago.

'Only if the occasion demands it,' he replied, turning her own words against her. He raised one eyebrow, obviously waiting for an answer.

Instinctively she shied away from discussing the events leading to her presence in Deer Creek. Perhaps if he'd come across as more sympathetic she would have mentioned her bout with infectious mononucleosis, and the lingering fatigue that plagued a small percentage of those recovering from the disease, but not now. She wouldn't give him any ammunition to use against her.

Hopefully, Hank hadn't mentioned her collapse in the emergency room. She crossed her fingers. 'What did Hank tell you?' she prevaricated.

'Nothing. I only heard of your arrival a few minutes before we were introduced.'

She hid her relief and assumed an air of nonchalance. 'I'm here because my boss sent me.'

'It doesn't make sense for Davenport to select his best physician for a stint at our hospital. He hasn't in the past.'

'Maybe he wants to foster a good relationship between our facilities.'

'If that was truly his objective he'd assign someone who wants to be in Deer Creek,' Adam said. 'Not an individual who's only putting in time until he or *she* —'

he glared at her '—can move on to bigger and better things.'

'So you're opposed to a person bettering him or herself?'

'No. However, I want some continuity. Patients don't become confident with their medical attention if they deal with a different physician each time they're ill.'

'In an emergency situation it wouldn't matter, would it?' she said, trying to be practical. 'After all, if a person is in a car accident and unconscious, will he really care?'

'He or she may not, but the family has to trust in the man or woman holding their loved one's life in his or her hands,' he insisted.

Sensing that his mind was unchangeable, she shrugged. 'Until the person you want appears on your doorstep you'll have to settle for me. Now, if you don't mind, Doctor,' she said in a dismissive tone, 'I have work to do.'

She gathered the clipboard and placed it in the crook of one arm just as Hank returned, his kindly, wrinkled face pensive. 'Is Adam answering your questions, Naomi?'

Although she'd been the one being cross-examined, rather than the one doing the asking, she didn't correct him. 'Yes, he is,' she said quietly. For the first time since she'd agreed to Davenport's suggestion she had misgivings over her decision. A few quiet weeks of isolation at her apartment suddenly held more appeal than dealing with someone as unbending as Adam Parker.

Hank looked both satisfied and relieved. 'Good. If you don't mind, I'll leave you now. Remember, Naomi, if you have any questions get in touch with one of us.'

'I will,' she promised.

'Did Eloise help you get settled in? I'm sorry I wasn't around much this weekend.'

She smiled. 'Your housekeeper is wonderful. Are you sure you want a boarder, though?'

Adam stared at Hank. 'A boarder?'

Hank looked pleased with himself. 'You've been telling me how I shouldn't rattle around all alone in my huge house so I'm sharing the place with our visiting doctors. It's more comfortable than the room the hospital provides.'

The dumbfounded look on Adam's face caused a smile to cross Naomi's lips, but she quickly steeled her face. It wouldn't do at all for him to see her amusement at his obvious bewilderment.

Hank patted her hand. 'Just make yourself at home, my dear. I'll see you later.'

As Hank left Lacey appeared on the threshold. 'Another ambulance is on its way, Dr Stewart. A crushing injury at the ice plant—a young man caught his arm in one of their machines.'

Her troubles with Adam Parker moved to the background. 'Alert Radiology for stat X-rays. Better notify the lab, too. I'll want blood crossmatched.' She turned to Adam. 'Do we have someone on staff who can deal with this sort of trauma?'

'Our general surgeon, Tyler Davis, has some orthopedic experience. He handles the minor emergencies but sends anything complicated to Kansas City. Lakeside, as a matter of fact, since they own us.'

Naomi pursed her lips. She perceived his distaste at the mention of the larger hospital's name and with his reference to ownership guessed that it stemmed from his unhappiness over the change in their independent status.

She'd delve into the situation later but for now the present medical emergency took precedence. She turned to Lacey. 'Get him. And notify a LifeWatch crew to stand by, as well.'

The nurse rushed away to place the phone calls.

'An airlift might not be necessary,' Adam said.

'Amputation may be his only option,' she admitted, 'but if it isn't the flight crew will be prepared to take off immediately.'

Naomi began to rummage through cabinets to double-check the location of supplies, but Adam forestalled her by placing his hand on her shoulder. The unexpected contact sent a trail of sparks down her body, causing her knees to weaken and make her feel decidedly feminine. How ironic that the only man who had engendered such an intense emotion was the same one who sought to discredit her.

'It could be rather messy,' he warned.

'Don't worry, I won't be shocked. I'm sure I've seen worse.'

He motioned to her dress. 'Maybe you should find something else to wear.'

She dug her hands into her lab coat pockets. 'I'd wanted to change but never had enough time.'

He quirked one eyebrow in disbelief but mercifully didn't comment. 'I'll stick around.'

Irritated by his intention to watch her every move, she clamped her teeth together. There was no point in assuring him of her capabilities—he wouldn't listen. Once again she had to prove her competence and she doubted if anything short of perfection would satisfy Adam Parker.

'Don't you have patients to see?'

'I've been on vacation for a week. Another hour or two won't matter.'

Naomi shrugged as she opened a cabinet marked IV Supplies. 'Suit yourself.'

He crossed his arms. 'What? No argument?'

She closed the doors. 'I don't have the time or the inclination. For the record, I don't appreciate you looking over my shoulder. I'll warn you, though. If you get in my way I won't have any qualms about calling Security to throw you out of my department.'

His chuckle was deep and hearty and his eyes twinkled with laughter.

'I'm glad you're amused,' she snapped. Her threat was obviously no threat at all.

'Sorry,' he said, clearly unrepentant. 'You haven't met our daytime security guard, have you?'

A sinking feeling came over her. 'No.'

'Wally Ochs is twenty-two years old, five feet six, about a hundred and twenty pounds and has the personality of a lovable puppy. I don't think he'll be much help to you.'

It figures, she thought. 'What do you do if an unruly patient or relative causes problems?'

Adam shrugged. 'We call the local police. For your information, Wally is the exception to our security staff. The others can handle anything that comes along.'

His pride was evident and her mouth twitched into a small smile. 'Even arrogant doctors?'

He raised one eyebrow. 'I imagine.'

'Then I'll have to wait for one of them to come on duty, won't I?' Stepping closer to the cabinets, she scanned the labels on the doors in search of the yellow disposable gowns intended to protect their clothing. Unfortunately her efforts were futile and she paused, trying to remember where she'd last seen the box.

Adam strode across the room, opened a cupboard and came back with two of the familiar paper-like garments in his hand. 'Is this what you're looking for?'

Noticing his tanned hands and fingers, she took the one he'd offered. 'Thanks,' she murmured, trying unsuccessfully to force the unbidden thoughts of his touch out of her mind. She thrust her arms through the sleeves and, out of the corner of one eye, watched Adam do the same. It was too easy to imagine him dressing— slipping a shirt over those broad shoulders, stepping into a pair of trousers.

Her hands fumbled with the strings at her neck and waist, much like the first time she'd ever gowned up to enter surgery. She purposely turned so that Adam wouldn't see her ineptitude and scolded herself for her unprofessional reaction.

Lacey returned a moment later. 'Dr Davis is in surgery, but he'll be here as soon as he finishes.'

The nurse's presence seemed to ground the charged atmosphere of personal awareness and Naomi felt herself released from its magnetic hold. 'Let's hope it won't be long,' she said, relieved to concentrate on business.

'Radiology is bringing their portable unit now and a lab technician is on the way.'

Naomi nodded with satisfaction. 'The only thing missing is our patient.'

The familiar emergency siren wailed in the distance. 'That's him,' Lacey answered, hurrying to meet the ambulance crew at the loading dock.

Naomi whipped a pair of latex gloves from the box

on the counter and followed, pulling them over her hands as she rushed to keep up.

Once again Dale and Rich accompanied their patient, this time a twenty-eight-year-old male with an oxygen mask over his face.

Naomi listened to their recitation of vital signs, noting the high pulse rate and the low blood pressure as she saw the red bandages on his mangled forearm. Soft tissue injuries were a given; the question was how badly the bones were crushed and if the blood supply to his hand had been cut off.

'CBC, crossmatch for four units, chem-six and a blood gas,' she ordered as the group maneuvered the gurney toward the trauma room. 'Start another IV with Ringer's lactate. Use a large-bore needle.' Fluid replacement was critical to keep him from going into shock.

She felt for the radial pulse in the man's wrist. When she found it the tell-tale thump was faint. His fingers were cold, but as she pressed on the nail beds they turned from white to pink in a few seconds. In spite of the damage, her patient hadn't lost all circulation and she upgraded her prognosis.

'How bad is it?' the fellow asked, his face etched with pain and his voice faint over the hiss of oxygen.

'We'll know after we run a few tests and take some pictures,' she said as the group brought the gurney to its destination.

Naomi leaned close to the man's ear. 'What's your name?'

'Kevin. Warner.' He gasped. 'Damn, it hurts.'

'I know. We're going to give you something right now for the pain. Are you allergic to any medications?'

He closed his eyes and grimaced. 'No.'

'Demerol, please,' she told Lacey. 'Is Radiology ready?'

'Right here,' a technician, standing in the background, said.

'I need A, P and lateral views,' she said, using the familiar anterior and posterior initials for brevity's sake. 'Lacey, call LifeWatch. Monitor—'

Adam interrupted. 'Wait,' he told the nurse, before addressing Naomi, 'aren't you jumping the gun? You may not need LifeWatch.'

Naomi felt his pulse. It was faint, but still there. 'I think we will.'

He moved closer until they stood shoulder to shoulder. 'Our surgeon may disagree.'

'You said yourself that Dr Davis doesn't handle complicated bone injuries.'

'He may decide it's best to amputate.'

She met his gaze. 'Then it's a good thing he isn't making the decision.'

'Flying him out of here isn't like a quick trip upstairs in an elevator. We're talking a half an hour, minimum.'

'I know.'

'Kevin may not make it if we don't do something now.'

Naomi didn't hesitate. 'He's young. He will.'

'What makes you so certain? I've known him and his family for years and I don't want to tell his wife that we lost him because of a physician's grandstand gesture.'

His tone was as sharp as his words, but she refused to lose her temper. Secure in the knowledge that this was *her* patient and that the situation was within *her* specialty of emergency medicine, she ignored Adam to give Tim an order. 'Monitor his blood pressure and pulse every five minutes.'

Tim followed her instructions, his interest in the unfolding clash unmistakable. Naomi faced Adam. How she handled this confrontation with the local physician in front of these bystanders would affect her relationships with the staff. She couldn't—*wouldn't*—work where someone questioned her every diagnosis.

'And I don't want to tell his wife that we could have saved his arm but didn't. The bleeding has slowed and he has circulation to his hand. Check for yourself.'

She moved slightly to allow him access to the damaged extremity.

He edged his way closer until his elbow brushed against her side, his woodsy masculine aftershave counterbalancing the distinctive smell of blood and the sterile odors of the emergency room. His gloved hands felt for Warner's radial pulse and silence filled the room as everyone stood stock-still, waiting for his verdict.

'So,' she said, her voice firm, 'what will it be? Or do you intend to waste more time arguing?' Once again she met his gaze, unflinching.

Several more tense seconds passed.

'Lacey,' he finally said, the dark pupils of his eyes still focused on Naomi's, 'you heard Dr Stewart's orders.'

The collective tension in the room seemed to dissipate and Naomi stifled a sigh of relief. Lacey rushed from the room and everyone sprang into action with their respective assignments.

By the time Kevin's wife arrived the X-rays had confirmed what Naomi had already suspected—Kevin had major soft-tissue damage and his radius and ulna were crushed.

'What are his chances?' Luann Warner asked Adam. Her face was pale and her eyes were red-rimmed but, to her credit, she remained calm.

Naomi glanced at the physician and waited for his reply. Although she would have preferred to answer the question herself, she understood the woman's need to be reassured by her trusted family doctor.

'He's stable,' Adam said.

'His arm?'

Adam hesitated. 'We'll do our best, but I can't make any promises.' He glanced at Naomi. 'No one can.'

Naomi caught his warning note and chafed under his censure. Although she'd never intended to guarantee that Kevin's arm would be restored to its pre-accident condition, she was cautiously optimistic.

'I understand.' Luann's voice wavered.

Before Mrs Warner could ask anything else the fifty-year-old surgeon strode in, still wearing his sweat-darkened green surgical suit and cap.

'What do we have?' Dr Davis asked, edging his way to the gurney.

Naomi related her findings and decision as he studied the X-ray films, his face grim. At last he spoke. 'I doubt if anyone can save it,' he warned, peering over his glasses at Naomi.

A muffled gasp came from Mrs Warner and she gripped her husband's uninjured hand to her chest.

Naomi held firm. 'I've seen Dr McAllister work miracles before. This patient deserves a chance for one of his own, doesn't he?'

Dr Davis looked thoughtful. 'What do you think?'

he asked Kevin. 'Can you handle a trip to the big city?'

Kevin managed a weak grin at the same time his wife murmured, 'Oh, yes.'

Dr Davis patted Kevin's shoulder and chuckled. 'I didn't think you'd argue.'

A young nursing aide rushed in. 'The chopper is here,' she announced, her eyes wide with excitement from the drama.

'Is everything organized?' Naomi asked. At Lacey's confirmation, she pressed on, 'The lab reports, the X-rays, the units of blood?'

'All accounted for,' Lacey said.

Within a short time the LifeWatch team hurried into the room, assessed their patient and were on their way outside to the small helipad on the hospital's east lawn.

'Sorry there isn't room for you,' the flight nurse said to Mrs Warner as the entourage approached the helicopter. 'We'll take good care of him.'

Luann's smile was a trifle wan. 'I know.' She stared down at her groggy husband and leaned over to graze her lips against his cheek and brush at the lock of dark hair plastered onto his forehead. 'I'll see you when you wake up,' she told her husband as a tear trickled down her cheek.

She stepped back and the crew slid him inside. A few minutes after the staff and pilot took their seats the rotors revved to high decibel levels.

The wind currents whipped tendrils of Naomi's hair free and she tucked them behind her ears. The steady 'thwop-thwop' of the blades grew into a whir and she offered a silent prayer for Kevin's recovery as the chopper slowly rose off the ground.

Although his condition was stable and she had faith

in both the LifeWatch crew and the surgical staff at Lakeside, the unexpected was always possible. If anything happened. . . She shuddered to think about how it would affect her future at Deer Creek.

The helicopter cleared the elm trees and headed southward, causing a collective sigh among the spectators. Naomi glanced at Adam. His jaw was set and his eyebrows had formed a thick line, but before she could look away he pinned his steely gaze on her. Although he didn't say a word, his thoughts were evident. He would hold her personally responsible if Kevin Warner suffered an early demise.

In the next instant he turned his attention to Luann. 'Do you have a ride to Kansas City?' he asked, steering her toward the hospital with an arm around her shoulders.

'My brother will drive me,' she said. 'My mom's keeping the kids.'

'Good.' Adam sounded satisfied. 'If you need anything, let me know.'

'I will,' Luann promised.

Following behind, Naomi suddenly felt extraneous although she didn't know why. She loved emergency work, partly due to the excitement and partly because contact with family members was limited; once she'd stabilized the patient she turned him or her over to someone else for long-term care. It was all nice and neat, and she maintained a polite distance with the people she treated, even with those few who regularly visited the ER.

Today, however, *she* wanted to be the one giving Luann Warner moral support, which didn't make sense at all.

She was tired, she decided as she passed through the electronic doors at the ambulance entrance. The stress of a new job, running at full speed from the moment she'd arrived—plus dealing with Adam Parker—had caused this strange shift in her emotions. After she'd settled in she'd be more like her old self.

But first she had to discuss a few things with Dr Parker. She squared her shoulders and marched forward, intent on catching him before he left.

Naomi rounded the corner and saw him at the nurses' station several yards away with the telephone receiver to his ear. She approached at a near jog and heard him say, 'I'm on my way.'

He handed the receiver to Lacey and took two long strides toward the swinging doors separating the emergency services department from the main hospital corridor.

'Dr Parker.' Naomi raised her voice. 'I'd like a word with you.'

Adam stopped with one hand on the door and turned toward her. 'Is it more important than a two-year-old having a seizure?'

She blinked. 'No.'

'Then I'll be on Paeds. You can handle things here, can't you?' He raised one eyebrow.

His attitude grated on her nerves but she smiled through clenched teeth. 'It'll be tough but I'll do my best.'

Her irony apparently wasn't lost on him because his mouth twitched. 'See that you do,' he said before he disappeared from view.

The doors swished to a gentle stop while Naomi

thrust her hands into her pockets, balled them into fists and mentally counted to ten.

'He can be rather infuriating at times,' Lacey commented in an offhanded manner.

Naomi took a deep breath. 'You mean he knows how to be personable?'

Lacey laughed. 'It doesn't seem like it today, but he is more often than not. He gives a hundred and ten per cent to his patients and expects everyone else to do the same. Woe to those who don't.'

At least they had something in common, even though he didn't realize it, Naomi thought.

'He's really a nice guy.'

'I'll have to take your word for it,' Naomi said, voicing her skepticism.

'Just give him a chance. He wasn't too thrilled with the idea of merging with Lakeside since our grandfather established this hospital, but he knows the advantages of such a change.'

Naomi's stomach flip-flopped. 'Wait a minute. You said "our grandfather". You're related?'

Lacey grinned. 'He's my older brother—'

Naomi's shoulders slumped. Dropping her chin to her chest, she rubbed the back of her neck.

'—but don't hold it against me.'

Naomi raised her head and managed a weak smile. 'You don't look anything like him.'

'I take after our mother's side of the family. I've also been married so my name didn't give you a clue. Don't feel badly. Newcomers usually don't make the connection.'

Struck by the significance of Adam's sister working

in ER—Lakeside's trouble spot—Naomi studied the younger woman.

As if Lacey had read Naomi's mind, she added, 'I wasn't assigned to the ER while Dr Carothers was here. When I took over this position Dr Montgomery had already earned his reputation and was on his way out. Most of what I know is secondhand information.' She cleared her throat. 'Which I won't repeat.'

Reassured by Lacey's attitude, Naomi leaned against the chest-high counter and rested her arms on the smooth Formica surface. 'Are there any other relatives I should know about?' If she had to tread softly around Dr Parker's entire family the next three months could be worse than a jail sentence.

'My aunt, Rachel, is in charge of Medical Records. My cousin, Karen, is the head dietician and another cousin runs the laundry service.'

'In other words, make sure my charts are up to date, rave about the food and don't complain about the sheets. Right?'

Lacey laughed. 'You know, I think you're just what Adam needs.'

'Which is?'

'Someone who has a sense of humor and isn't afraid to stand up to him. He's got so used to his word being law, both at the hospital and at home, that it will do him good to become acquainted with the concept of compromise.'

'I'm only staying for three months. Not nearly enough time for your brother to master the nuances of this particular subject.'

'Maybe, but somehow I doubt it.'

'So he rules his home with an iron fist, too. What's his wife like?'

'Oh, he's not married. He's too busy running our lives.' Lacey rose, took a few steps to the coffee station in the corner and lifted the glass pot off the warmer. 'Want some?'

'Half a cup, please.'

She filled a styrofoam cup to the requested amount and handed it to Naomi.

'Thanks.' Naomi skirted the counter and sat in a stenographer's chair behind the desk, before sipping the steaming drink. 'Back up. What do you mean about Adam running your life?' Learning about the 'enemy' wasn't gossiping, she told herself; it was self-preservation.

'Dad died when we were kids. Adam had just been accepted at medical school at the time and, being the oldest, he took his "head of the family" responsibilities seriously. He was all set to find a job instead but Hank, who was my father's partner, convinced him to continue with his studies. Adam finished med school, came home and, although we're no longer the teenagers we once were, he still feels it's his duty to watch over us. Which, I might add, he does with a great deal of enthusiasm.'

'And you don't like it?'

Lacey sighed. 'There are times when it's nice. In general it's a real pain, having your brother act like a watchdog, if you know what I mean.'

Naomi shook her head. The concept was intriguing but, in her experience, totally foreign. 'Sorry. My parents are both gone now and my brother is a career Navy man. We keep in touch, but I don't see him very often.'

'What about grandparents? Aunts, uncles, cousins?'

'Not a one. Just a few friends who are like sisters.'

Lacey sighed. 'It must be nice not having to answer to anyone. Even if my sisters and I didn't have Adam, we have enough relatives in town who delight in sticking their noses in our business.'

'There are good and bad points to every situation,' Naomi said. Like volunteering to work all the holidays because she felt guilty if her co-workers with families were separated from their children while she was home alone.

'At least you didn't have someone screening every male who asked you out.'

Considering the predicaments young people got themselves in, Naomi thought it a nice idea. But she held in her comments as Lacey continued.

'None of us dated much because Adam intimidated the guys. I think that's why I had a whirlwind courtship with Bill. We had to sneak out to see each other because Adam didn't approve.' She shrugged. 'Looking back, I can see why the two of them didn't get along but, to Adam's credit, he didn't say "I told you so" when our marriage disintegrated.'

'And now that you're divorced?'

Lacey studied the floral design on her coffee-mug. 'He thinks I should go out again.'

'And what do you think?' Naomi asked diplomatically.

Lacey's face turned pink but she didn't comment.

'There is someone, isn't there?' Before Lacey could answer Naomi recalled the last time she'd seen the nurse blush. 'Dale, perhaps?'

Lacey grinned as she shrugged. 'Yeah.'

'He seems like a nice fellow.'

'He is.' Lacey fell silent.

'But you're not ready,' Naomi guessed.

'Not for anything serious, and I'm afraid Dale wants more than a platonic relationship.'

'Then the next time he asks you out make it clear how you feel. If he's not willing to give you the time and space he'll move on to someone else.'

Lacey thought a moment. 'Sounds simple enough. I'll do it.' She studied Naomi. 'You're so matter-of-fact. Has this happened to you?'

Naomi smiled. 'Not really. My career is my life, and some men couldn't accept that. But I had to be honest about my goals—it was unfair to pretend otherwise.'

She rose and stretched, feeling somewhat rejuvenated. 'Thanks for the coffee. I think I'll take advantage of the momentary lull to change clothes. If I'm going to handle traumas I'd rather wear my uniform.'

For the rest of the day Naomi dealt with an assortment of minor complaints—conditions that a medical student could have handled—and learnt the layout of the hospital. She'd wondered if Adam would return to ER after he'd stabilized his pediatric patient but, as time elapsed, he didn't make an appearance. Her resolve strengthened with each passing hour—she wouldn't allow him to ignore her.

She debated tracking him down, then rejected the idea. He'd be back at some point, if for no other reason than to check on her work. And when he did she'd be prepared for verbal battle.

The end of her shift came as a welcome relief. She collected her gear from the physician's locker room and was on her way through the lounge when Adam strode through the door. She momentarily stopped in her tracks until his glance around the room landed on her.

Like a man on a mission, he made a beeline toward her and stopped in her path. Her stomach tensed.

'I just heard from Luann Warner,' he said without any preamble, his well-defined facial features impassive. 'Kevin went into cardiac arrest during surgery.'

CHAPTER THREE

SHOCKED by Adam's announcement, Naomi lost her grip on the duffel bag and canvas tote in her hands. They dropped onto the carpeting with a muffled thud just inches from her feet. Notebooks and manuals scattered across the floor but she ignored the disarray.

'I don't believe it. Are you sure?' she asked.

Adam nodded.

Hugging her purse to her chest, she sank onto the nearest chair and stared up at him. 'Kevin was doing so well. I was certain he wouldn't have any problems.'

'Well, he did.' Adam paused. 'Luckily, your Dr McAllister had two miracles in his pocket because not only did he pull Kevin through the arrest but he managed to save his arm.'

Sweet and welcome relief flooded over her. In the next instant, however, anger took hold and she narrowed her eyes. 'Why did you imply that something terrible had happened?'

'It did. A cardiac arrest isn't a minor condition,' Adam pointed out.

'You know what I mean.'

'You drew your own conclusions. Admit it. You were worried.'

Naomi crossed her arms. 'Concerned. Not worried.'

'Worried,' he corrected. 'If he had died your days in this institution would have been numbered and you knew it.'

Naomi shrugged, unwilling to give him the satisfaction of her agreement. 'They are anyway since I'm only assigned here through August.' She turned the subject back on the track she wanted. 'So Kevin's doing OK.'

'Barring any unexpected complications, yes.'

'I'm glad.' Remembering the reason she'd wanted to talk to him, she rose to avoid having him tower over her. He'd never accept her as an equal if she didn't minimize the physical distance between them. She slung her bag over her left shoulder, straightened her spine and mentally willed away her exhaustion.

'However, I don't appreciate having my orders countermanded. I'm not a medical student, needing constant supervision.'

'No, but you aren't used to the way we do things around here. You're not in Kansas City any more.'

'I'm well aware of my location,' she said in a calm, authoritative voice. 'What I don't understand is why you were unwilling to airlift him out of Deer Creek. If you'd examined him earlier you'd have known he couldn't stay here—'

'Contrary to what you believe, I wasn't anxious for the man to lose his arm,' Adam interrupted. 'There are a lot of factors to be weighed when transporting a patient. Each option comes with its own set of unique risks. I had to see if you knew what you were doing.'

'It was a test?' she asked, incredulous. How inconceivable and degrading to have this man treat her not as a well-trained colleague but as a greenhorn subordinate. 'Gee, did I pass?'

Adam raised one eyebrow at her thinly veiled sarcasm but didn't comment. 'I once had a patient in a somewhat similar situation. Unfortunately, the outcome was the opposite of Kevin Warner's. I'd rather have my patient alive with one arm than dead with both of them.'

She should have suspected that a previous incident had made him cautious—she, too, often relied on her own personal experiences when making decisions. Even so, his methods left a lot to be desired.

'I'm always willing to discuss treatment options. However, the operative word is "discuss".'

'I'll keep that in mind,' he said wryly.

As she bent down to stuff the notebooks back in her tote she doubted that he would. A man who was used to his word being law, both in his private and professional life, couldn't change his character overnight. Yet it was a small concession, and for the moment it was better than the distrust she'd encountered on their first meeting.

Naomi stood, balancing her bags in both hands. With her first step forward the strap of her purse slid off one shoulder. The sudden shift upset her balance and she stumbled.

Adam grabbed for her bags. His eyes narrowed slightly and a speculative expression crossed his face.

'I can take them,' she insisted, retaining her grip on the handles in spite of his hold on them. The heat from his hands and the potency of his pine-woods aftershave sent a shiver of awareness through her.

'You're exhausted. You can barely carry yourself.'

She stiffened at his blunt but accurate remark. 'I'm fine. And if I'm tired it's understandable. Moving into a new community, settling into a new apartment and learning the ropes of a new job—all within forty-eight hours—is stressful for anyone.'

'Point taken. But since I'm leaving anyway I'll walk you to your car.'

Considering his earlier hostility, the offer startled her. To be honest, she wasn't certain that she had enough energy left for a verbal sparring match. 'Do I need an escort in broad daylight?'

He shrugged, giving her a half-smile. 'Deer Creek is safe enough. Unlike the big city, chivalry hasn't died here.'

As she hurried to keep up with his long strides across the room a thought occurred to her. 'I didn't park in the doctors' lot.' At his look of surprise she added, 'I refused to risk having my car towed because I'd violated someone's established parking tradition.'

His expression became amused, as if he understood that *he* was the person she'd been concerned about. 'The stalls for physicians are marked, but we function on a first come, first served basis. Feel free to use whichever space is available. For your own information, we don't have authorization stickers because the security staff recognizes our vehicles. Yours won't be bothered—one of the many advantages to small town living.'

She heard the pride in his voice. He obviously enjoyed life in Deer Creek. 'That's comforting.'

Tucking her tote bag under his left arm, he opened the door and waited for her to pass by. For all his perceived arrogance, she couldn't fault his manners.

'How's your pediatric patient doing? The one with seizures.'

'I'm not sure. He's never had any problems before. We did a full battery of tests, including a spinal tap, but nothing showed up out of the ordinary.'

'What about the CT scan and MRI?'

'The portable units won't be here until Thursday.'

Three days from now. 'Can you wait until then?' she asked. The prospect of not having sophisticated diagnostic equipment available at a moment's notice was daunting, and would require some thought adjustment on her part.

'No. I've sent him to Kansas City. I would have preferred calling David McCary at the medical school. . .' His voice died and his mouth formed hard line.

She could understand his displeasure. Building a rapport with specialists took time and he obviously had confidence in his referral physicians. Unfortunately, under the terms of the Lakeside-Deer Creek merger, all cases had to be transferred to someone on the larger hospital's staff.

No exceptions.

'Dr Chin is outstanding,' she said, hoping that her opinion would alleviate some of his worries. 'He keeps a close eye on the residents in his service.'

'Let's hope so.'

The corridor branched ahead and she slowed her pace, trying to remember if the right or left passage would lead them to the front entrance.

'Left,' he ordered, as if realizing her uncertainty.

They passed by the accounting offices and the main reception area. The tweed fabric covering the sofas and chairs showed no signs of wear and co-ordinated with the pastel-colored wall-coverings. The glass and chrome sparkled, the wood shone with its high gloss and a lemony fresh scent filled the air.

'Your environmental services people do a nice job,'

she commented as they crossed the expanse to reach the entrance. 'You should be proud of your hospital.'

'The whole community is.'

The automatic doors rumbled as they slid apart and a blast of heat hit her before she stepped outside. 'My car's over there. In the corner.' She pointed to the right as she walked in the direction she'd indicated, digging in her purse for the keys at the same time.

'What do you think of our ER department?' he asked.

'I'm not used to the organization, but it's equipped well enough. Here we are.' She came to a stop in front of a late-model royal blue Ford Mustang, feeling a measure of pride at the sight.

The sporty convertible, recently polished to a high shine, had been a birthday gift to herself a few months ago. After driving a vehicle that had seen better days long before it had come into her own possession as a college student, she'd saved her money and planned for the day she could own the car of her dreams.

She unlocked the passenger door and swung it open. Turning toward Adam to retrieve her bags, she faltered at his expression.

His jaw was squared, his mouth was pressed into a hard line and his eyes were cool.

'Is something wrong?' she asked.

Adam's voice was like an ice cube—cold and hard. 'No. You just reminded me of something I'd forgotten for a few minutes.'

Whatever it was concerned her, although she didn't know what it might be. She hadn't meant her comments about the ER to be inflammatory, but had he taken offense at them?

He dropped the bags on the floorboard, then stepped back.

'Thanks,' she said, studying his reaction and feeling ill at ease.

'Get some rest,' he ordered, before turning away.

She stared at his retreating figure, amazed by the sudden change which had swept over him.

It would definitely be a long three months until she could go home.

Adam climbed into his Jeep Cherokee and slammed the door in disgust. The positive outcome of Kevin Warner's case had momentarily blinded him to Dr Stewart's shortcomings, but the sight of her brand-new expensive sports car brought him back to reality in an instant.

Recalling the dark circles under her eyes and the obvious slump to her shoulders, he gritted his teeth. 'Stress of a new job, huh,' he muttered to himself. 'Of course she's tired. She spent her last week in Kansas City, partying.'

At the same time, he couldn't fault the way she'd handled Kevin Warner's injuries. He recognized her expertise and knew that it was highly unlikely for her to develop her skills to that degree without a large investment of time and effort.

If only he didn't feel a connection, an invisible bond pulling them together. No matter what he called it he wouldn't allow it to hold him in its tentacles. He'd been blinded once by the wiles of a self-centered, power-hungry woman. It wouldn't happen again.

Feeling the need to unleash his frustration, he drove

toward Lacey's bungalow. In a few minutes he was pounding on her screen door.

Lacey appeared, wearing a sleeveless white shirt knotted at her midriff and a pair of dark blue denim shorts. A look of resignation crossed her face as she unlatched the hook. 'Adam. What a surprise.'

'Cut the sarcasm,' he said, stepping inside her living room and letting the door slam closed behind him. 'This is important.'

She sank into the nearest easy chair. 'I know why you're here. You want information on Dr Stewart.'

He perched on the edge of the sofa and, leaning forward, rested his elbows on his knees. 'Yes.'

Lacey folded her arms across her chest. 'You saw her in action. You don't need my impressions.'

Unfortunately he did. What he'd seen hadn't fitted his assessment of her character, and he wanted to resolve the discrepancy.

'Come on, Lace. Give me a break.'

'You won't like what I have to say.'

His stomach tensed. It was worse than he'd thought. 'I'm waiting.'

Lacey stared at him for a long minute. 'I won't be your spy.'

'I'm not asking you to be. I only want your opinion.'

She chewed on her lip, her face wrinkled with indecision. Finally she nodded. 'OK, but after this conversation ends I won't discuss the subject again. Is that clear?'

'Perfectly.'

'Mind you, I've only worked with her one day but Naomi Stewart seems to be a wonderful person.' Adam made a choking sound and she held up her hands. 'You asked for my opinion and I'm giving it. If you recall, I warned you less than thirty seconds ago.'

Adam clamped his teeth together. 'Go ahead.'

'She's also a great doctor. She's quick, she's thorough and I'm totally impressed. I know she's only temporary but I wish we could make a more permanent arrangement.'

'Forget it. Even if she's passed over for the promotion she won't stick around here. She's not the type.'

'And what type is that?'

Adam recognized the stubborn tilt to his sister's chin and the flinty gleam in her eyes. 'Naomi is used to the best. You can see it for yourself. She wears fancy clothes and designer perfume, drives an expensive sports car—'

'And what about the tailored suits in your own closet, brother dear?' Lacey tapped her forehead. 'Dare I mention the BMW in your garage, or the—?'

'OK, OK. The point is that Naomi Stewart is as out of place here as a hothouse rose in a wildflower patch.'

Lacey became thoughtful. 'I disagree. But if you do anything to make her leave before she's supposed to you'll create a riot.'

He gave her his give-me-a-break look. 'Oh, for Pete's sake—'

'I'm serious. And I'll be the instigator.'

The fierce expression on his sister's face gave Adam pause. Lacey had obviously accepted Naomi with open arms—a complete reversal of her attitude toward his former fiancée, Cynthia. In fact, Lacey and the others in his family had never said anything good or bad about Cynthia, making Lacey's defense of Naomi more surprising.

For a fleeting moment he wondered how the rest of his family would act once they met her. An introduction was inevitable—the town was too small for anyone to remain a stranger for long.

'Point taken. You haven't noticed anything unusual about her, have you?'

'What do you mean?'

'She looks pale. Washed-out. Exhausted.'

'I'm not surprised. Starting a new job is always stressful. I'd be dragging my feet, too, if I'd barely unpacked my suitcase and then worked a ten-hour day.'

Although Lacey's excuse mirrored Naomi's, Adam's doubts wouldn't be quietened. 'I'm still keeping my eye on her,' he said, leaning against the sofa cushions. 'If she's that tired she's bound to make mistakes. And, speaking of tired, have you seen Hank?'

'He needs a long rest,' Lacey agreed. 'We've been busy this past week so he deserves one.' Her expression became troubled. 'Now that you mention it, he's looked rather peaked the past few weeks. You don't think he's sick, do you?'

He drew a deep breath. 'I don't know. I've seen this coming for some time but whenever I talk to him about it he says he's fine. I've mentioned taking over more of the practice, but he insists on carrying his share of the load.'

'Hank won't slow down unless someone forces him. I want him around to see my kids when I have them someday. He's the closest thing to a grandfather they'll have.'

'He'll be great, won't he?' he asked, imagining the older man with toddlers, bearing an odd resemblance to Naomi Stewart, at his knee. 'Funny thing how time's slipping away. I thought I'd have several by now.'

'Me, too.' Her voice wavered.

Adam knew Lacey's divorce had taken away more than a husband—it had also killed her dreams of a hearth and home filled with children. 'Someday you will. When the time's right. Who knows? Dale may be just the—'

'Will you stop?' she protested.

He grinned. His teasing had been successful—her pensive expression had disappeared. 'For now.' He sniffed the air. 'What's cooking? Smells like—'

'My brownies!' She bounded to her feet and raced around the corner into the kitchen.

Adam followed and watched her yank open the oven door. Smoke billowed forth and once it had cleared he peered at the pan. The edges of the chocolate bar cookies had pulled away from the sides and resembled dark brown lava rock.

Using potholders, Lacey lifted the baking dish off the rack and placed it on top of the stove. 'They're ruined!'

He pressed on the center with an index finger. 'The middle can be salvaged. Can I have one?'

'Absolutely not. These aren't for you.' She tossed the hot pads to one side of the stove.

Knowing her penchant for keeping snack food—especially desserts—out of her house, Adam stared down at her and caught a whiff of her Calvin Klein fragrance—a scent she only wore on special occasions.

'Ah,' he said as understanding dawned. 'Company's coming.'

'No. Yes.' She wiped her forehead with the back of her hand. 'Sort of.'

'For you to be this rattled, it has to be a guy,' Adam decided. 'Who is it?'

'None of your business.' Lacey glanced at the clock. 'Shoot. Now I don't have time to mix another batch.'

Adam snapped his fingers. 'Dale. It's got to be Dale.'

She stiffened. 'What makes you say that?'

He grinned. 'He's the only one who's been asking you out. So you finally said yes.'

'Don't make a big deal out of it.'

'I was right. It *is* Dale.'

'A lucky guess, Dr Watson. Do you have a problem with him?' She placed her hands on her hips and her eyes gleamed with defiance.

Adam held up his hands. 'Hey, he's a nice guy.' A thought occurred to him and he leaned against the counter. 'How long have you been seeing each other?'

'If you must know, this is our first date. Naomi said I should tell him that I wasn't ready for anything serious and so, when I saw him in the cafeteria at lunchtime, I did.' She looked sheepish. 'Next thing I knew, my evening had been planned.'

Adam wasn't sure that he liked Naomi Stewart's influence over his sister, but if Lacey was prepared to risk going on a date he couldn't complain.

'He'll be here soon,' she said.

'And you want me to leave. I understand.' He studied Lacey's outfit. 'You look—'

'Before you comment please remember I've been choosing my clothes for a number of years. You may not have noticed but I'm an adult now.'

'Great,' he finished, revising his sentence. 'Very nice.'

'That's better.' She gave him a gentle shove and

he allowed her to usher him into the living room.

'Have fun.'

'I will. Goodbye.'

Adam stopped at the front door, covering up his protective nature with gentle teasing. 'Maybe I should stay and say hello. It would be the polite thing to do.'

'Adam.' Her tone was warning.

He grinned. 'I'm going. I've screened your dates for so long that it's hard to stop.'

'Force yourself. If you can't, go pick on Evelyn or Melissa or Amy. I'll see you tomorrow.'

With a jaunty wave, Adam left. Yet, as he drove away, his doubts about Naomi Stewart bobbed to the surface again. True, there were logical explanations for his observations, but his instincts suggested that there was something not quite right about Ms Stewart.

'Give her enough rope and she'll hang herself,' he said, quoting one of Hank's familiar adages.

It took a few days to settle back into his routine, and at the end of the third day Adam headed for his partner's familiar Tudor-style house on Birchwood Lane, hoping for a private moment with his mentor.

He'd always considered Hank's place as much 'home' as his own parents', and in times past he'd usually knocked a few times and then walked in as he'd called out his greetings. This time, however, he pressed the doorbell button.

By the time the Westminster chimes had faded Hank had appeared with his billfold in hand. 'I thought you were the paperboy.' He tucked the wallet in his back pocket and stepped aside for Adam to enter.

'Nope. Just me. I didn't think your boarder would

appreciate coming across an unannounced visitor,'
Adam pointed out. 'I dropped by because I was hoping
for a quiet visit to catch up on what's been happening.'

'Naomi's arrival has been the big event of the week,
but that's already old news. I want to hear all about
your vacation with your friends,' Hank said, heading
through the house toward the kitchen. 'The last time I
went to the mountains was. . .' he paused, squinting one
eye in thought '. . .fifteen years ago. At least.'

'We hiked into the mountains, rode the ski lift and
did all the usual touristy things people do when they go
to Aspen, Colorado.' As they passed the stairs leading to
the floor above Adam recognized Naomi's elusive
scent, intermingling with Hank's Old Spice cologne
and the housekeeper's lavender toilet water. He glanced
around, expecting Naomi to appear.

'Too bad you missed Naomi,' Hank said, removing
two glass tumblers from the cupboard.

From long habit, Adam grabbed a pitcher of freshly
squeezed lemonade from the refrigerator—Eloise
replenished it daily—and a tray of ice from the freezer.
He carried everything to the counter and dropped the
cubes into the glasses. 'Where'd she go?'

Hank poured the lemonade and handed Adam a cup.
'Shopping. She said something about needing a birthday
card. I sent her downtown.'

Adam took a long swallow. Remembering Cynthia's
hoot of derision at their local merchants' limited selection of goods, in comparison to what she was
accustomed, he winced.

'Too sour?' Hank asked.

He shook his head. 'It's fine.'

Hank pulled one of the padded chairs away from the

small breakfast table and sat down. 'What do you think of Naomi?'

From the look of excitement on Hank's face, he definitely shared Lacey's sentiments. Although Adam had his doubts, he didn't want to dash Hank's high spirits. 'It's too soon to say,' he prevaricated. 'I only met her.'

'Oh, come on. Admit it, she'll be an asset to us.'

'It's hard to judge her from one case.' Two, he mentally corrected. He still planned to look into Chester Lang's demise.

Hank waved his hand. 'She's good and you know it.'

Adam let the comment pass. Since he hadn't come to discuss the newest addition to their staff he steered the conversation in another direction. 'I hear you've had a rough week.'

Hank's smile was half-hearted. 'Lack of sleep comes with the territory. I'm not getting any younger either.'

'None of us are. Have you given any more thought to slowing down? Working part time?'

'I've been considering it. But I won't do it at your expense.'

'I'll start looking for someone to ease gradually into the practice. In the meantime, I can cover—'

'Absolutely not. You will not pick up the slack.' Hank was adamant. 'When we find another physician I'll cut back my hours. Not before.'

'That could take several years. Residents are already spoken for, and even if we recruited a medical student today they'd have to finish their training. I don't want you running yourself into the ground.'

'Neither do I.' Hank raised the glass to his mouth and drank deeply. 'That hits the spot,' he said, before he continued in an offhanded tone, 'There might be someone who'd help us out.'

'No kidding?' Locums were usually booked far in advance. 'Anyone I know?'

Hank nodded. 'Naomi Stewart.'

CHAPTER FOUR

ADAM stared at Hank in dismay. 'What makes you think Naomi would be interested?'

'She may not be,' Hank admitted, 'but she's the only doctor who's readily available. Covering the ER on a call basis isn't ideal, but she might be willing to juggle both positions.'

'Yes, but. . .'

Hank took a long swallow of lemonade. 'It's just an idea. Nothing's definite. In fact, I haven't mentioned this to anyone yet. You're the first.'

'You actually want to turn your patients over to a total stranger? Someone we don't know anything about?'

'You're always so cautious, Adam. Too cautious sometimes. It may seem as if I'm making a snap decision, but I'm not. I've thought about this for a long time.'

Adam rested his arms on the table and clutched his glass with both hands. 'I'll phone the locums we usually work with. Maybe they're free.'

Hank shook his head. 'I've already checked. Other than a day or two here and there, they're booked.'

Adam stared at Hank's face, noting every line carved by age and responsibility. If Hank had tried to find someone to take over part of his load then he was definitely serious about easing into retirement. 'You really have faith in her, don't you?'

Hank pursed his lips as he nodded. Finally he spoke.

'Did you know that she's the same age my Carrie would be if she'd lived? Carrie wanted to be a doctor, too.'

Adam remembered Hank's only child and the suffering the family had endured during her battle with a defective heart. He'd been sixteen at the time and little Carrie had been like one of his younger sisters. Hank's wife, Angela, had died a few years later from breast cancer.

Hank's gaze didn't waver. 'Naomi isn't Carrie and I know that, but I see some of Carrie's personality in Naomi. My reasons aren't logical but in my gut I trust Naomi. Regardless, if you object the discussion is closed.'

Adam stared at the man who'd helped him through the loss of his father, supported him through medical school and encouraged him through much of his life. Now it was his turn to do something for the man who'd given of himself so selflessly in the past—the same man who'd continue to do so without argument if Adam said the all-powerful word 'no'.

In that split second Adam knew that he couldn't protest. He still had qualms about the plan involving Naomi Stewart, but Hank's current needs outweighed his reservations.

He'd do anything for Hank Taylor, even if it meant sharing his patient load with Naomi Stewart.

'If she's the one you want then ask her,' Adam said. 'But she'll refuse.'

'Probably. But I'm counting on you to convince her.'

'*Me*? You don't need me.'

Hank bobbed his head. 'You're part of the package. If we're united she can't possibly turn us down.'

*   *   *

From the time Naomi saw Hank and Adam walk into the trauma room where she was examining the defibrillator she sensed that something monumental was about to happen. However, she'd never expected an offer to join their private practice.

Even now, she could tell that he was uncomfortable with the idea. His expression was guarded, his jaw squared. He shifted his weight, tugged on the collar of his shirt and crossed his arms as if impatient.

For Adam Parker, asking for her assistance was probably the most unpleasant task he'd faced in a long time. The thought nearly made her smile, but she clamped her lips together to keep it from reaching her mouth.

'We're asking for a limited commitment of a few days a week,' Adam said in a cool tone, 'and only until we locate someone who's willing to stay long-term. I'm already making enquiries.'

She kept her face impassive as she considered the repercussions of her decision. If she agreed, her stint with them would be brief—Adam wouldn't rest until he'd found a suitable replacement.

While she'd filled in at various clinics before on her days off to help a colleague in a tight situation, those times had been rare and only for physicians with whom she'd built a good rapport. Never for anyone who barely tolerated her presence.

'What about the ER coverage?' she asked.

'Rather than being on duty, you'll be on call for those situations that Lacey, our nurse practitioner, and the physician's assistant can't handle.'

'How do the other doctors feel about this arrangement?' she asked.

'As long as you're available during the hours we've

already set forth, they don't object. Since I'll be in the office myself it shouldn't pose too great a problem in the event you have to leave for the hospital.'

Hank and Adam had thought of everything. Part of her wanted to accept—to be a part of this closely knit community for a short time. Yet she was eager to go home and leave Deer Creek behind—she had a multitude of reasons for doing so.

First of all, she preferred emergency medicine— patch 'em up and send 'em on—over general practice. The nature of the job itself prevented her from forming personal attachments. Relationships remained on a professional level and no one came too close for her comfort.

Nor was she reminded of the missing elements of her life, elements that her childhood friends—Beth and Kirsten—now had. The losses she'd suffered in her lifetime—her family, her dear friend Ellen McGraw, a few special patients—had taught her to keep her relationships casual. Colleagues and co-workers considered her a loner but, in her mind, being one was a small price to pay to avoid heartache.

Finally, she had a more compelling reason to refuse. Practicing medicine meant everything to her and the sooner she returned to Lakeside the sooner she could resume the uphill climb on her career ladder. She still napped every evening, but the bone-numbing exhaustion was gone. A few more weeks of light duty and she'd be in fighting form once again.

She wouldn't do anything to delay her recovery. For that reason alone she justified her decision.

She started to shake her head to refuse the offer, but at the sight of Hank's hopeful expression she couldn't.

The kindly doctor had opened his home to her and it didn't seem right to repay him in such a cold manner and without any explanations. Yet she refused to give any.

Hank was the only person in Deer Creek who knew about the events leading to her presence here and she wanted to keep it that way. She was too proud to announce the truth, especially to Adam Parker, but citing 'personal reasons' as an excuse seemed lame. His opinion of her was already jaded, and without suitable grounds she'd appear self-centered as well. After all, how could a physician refuse to help a colleague in a time of need?

A suspicion grew and her eyes narrowed. Hank Taylor, for all his sweetness, wasn't above manipulating people.

'I don't think Davenport will complain if we use you in another capacity,' Hank said.

With a sinking heart Naomi realized that Hank had a point. Her mission was to make the merger sail through the troubled waters—to meet the needs of Deer Creek's physicians. Her boss didn't care how it was accomplished.

Davenport had also insisted that she was to use the entire summer to recuperate. He'd made it clear before she'd left Kansas City that he didn't want to see her before September, and she'd never known him to change his mind. Still, it wouldn't hurt to try. . .

'Your offer is flattering, but I can't give you an answer without discussing this with Dr Davenport,' Naomi said, trying to leave some means to escape this new twist in her life. Surely, after she'd cited her reasons as eloquently as possible, her boss wouldn't give his blessing.

'Of course,' Hank said smoothly. 'Talk it over with Walter. Then let us know.'

Chewing on her lower lip, she glanced at Adam. He wore a bored expression, as if he'd known that her response would be negative. No matter what decision she made, Adam Parker wouldn't be happy.

Luckily, Parker's likes and dislikes didn't matter to her. Davenport's did.

Adam cleared his throat. 'I want your answer as soon as possible. Preferably by Wednesday.'

His demand irritated her. 'Dr Davenport isn't easy to reach.'

He raised one eyebrow as if he didn't believe her. 'I'll be waiting,' he said. Immediately he strode away with his back ramrod-stiff.

Hank patted her arm. 'Take your time, dear.' He winked. 'Adam's temper grows short when he's worried. Don't let it bother you.'

Naomi studied him. Hank appeared pale and his mouth had a pinched look to it. He obviously had some sort of medical problem, which explained why Adam was in such a hurry for her reply. 'Have you had a recent physical?'

'A few weeks ago. At Lakeside.'

'Did they find anything?' She spoke softly.

He avoided her gaze. 'A slower pace will help.'

She picked up on his word choice. 'Help, but not cure?'

'The cure is more. . .' he hesitated '. . .involved.'

'Does Adam know?' Naomi suddenly forgave Hank for his sneaky orchestrations.

'No, and I don't want him to. He has enough to worry about without worrying over me.'

'Regardless—' she began.

'I'll tell him,' he interrupted, 'when and if it becomes necessary.'

'I won't say a word,' she promised. 'But if you need anything you know where to find me.' Sharing his home with her now took on a new meaning. 'Lucky thing we're under the same roof.'

Hank winked. 'From our first meeting I knew I could count on you.' With that, he saluted her and left.

A warm glow spread through her at his praise and for a few minutes she wondered if working in a family practice would be as bad as she'd originally thought.

'How did this happen?' Naomi studied her patient's hands and arms to ascertain the extent of the burns.

'I was working with a small bottle—about two hundred milliliters—of concentrated sulfuric acid under the fume hood.' The lab tech, Dana Mitchell, wore a hospital gown and dangled her bare legs as she sat on the exam table. Her medium-length carrot-colored hair hung in wet ringlets around her face.

'My hands felt slick but I didn't know why until I noticed a crack in the glass. When I examined the container to see if it was leaking the entire thing shattered in my hands. Acid ran down my arms and all over the counter before it started dripping onto the floor. By then my skin felt as if it was on fire so I yelled for help and immediately ran to the safety shower.'

'Smart thinking.' Naomi gently turned Dana's palms down to examine the back of her hands.

Dana winced. 'That hurts. How bad is it?'

Naomi considered for a moment. Dana's skin was red and several moist blisters had started to form, indicating that the damage had gone into the dermis. Her increased sensitivity to stimuli and the good capillary refill, however, pointed to an excellent prognosis.

'Most of this is superficial—a first-degree burn. The blisters indicate spots where the burn is deeper, but those areas are small and should heal nicely.'

Naomi glanced at her feet and legs. The skin appeared slightly reddened, with only minimal injury. Using the 'rule of nines', where the total surface area for second- and third-degree burns is calculated based on the portion of the body affected, she assessed the extent of Dana's injuries at the moment as three per cent. 'You were lucky.'

Lacey walked in, carrying a huge three-ring note- book. 'Here are the material safety data sheets. I've flagged the one for sulfuric acid.'

'Thanks.' Manufacturers were required by law to sup- ply users with information relating to the hazards of their products and medical treatment if an exposure occurred. As part of the hospital's safety program the emergency services department kept an MSDS form on file for all chemicals used on hospital property. With the information only a fingertip away, staff members were ensured prompt and appropriate medical attention in situations such as this.

Lacey laid the oversized binder on the bed and opened it to the appropriate place. Naomi scanned the pages for any new or unusual instructions and found nothing to contradict what she'd been taught.

'Will I have to stay in the hospital?' Dana asked, lines of worry etching her forehead.

'A rule of thumb is to treat partial thickness burns as an outpatient, provided they don't exceed fifteen to twenty per cent of the total body surface area. Chemical burns, however, can be tricky and are an exception,' Naomi said, trying to break the bad news gently. 'It may take several hours before we can determine the full extent of the damage. I won't send you home and risk complications. Plus, with your hands involved, you won't be able to care for yourself, anyway.'

Dana's shoulders slumped. 'I can't stay. My kids don't have a place to go.'

'How old are they?'

'Allie is four and Catrina is six.'

Too young to help their mother with the most basic tasks. 'You won't be able to do much for them. You'll have to keep your hands and arms clean, dry and elevated. The dressing must be changed twice a day and an antibiotic ointment applied each time as well. How will you manage?'

'My girls don't have anyone else but me. I can't leave them alone.'

Naomi's resolve softened under Dana's desperation. She glanced at Lacey who also wore a pleading expression. Before she knew it she'd changed her mind to go against accepted practice.

'We haven't been busy today so we can get by without using this room for a while. Wouldn't you agree, Lacey?'

The nurse's smile was broad. 'I'm certain of it.'

'In that case, we'll monitor you here in ER over the next few hours,' Naomi told Dana. 'If I don't see any change I'll reconsider my earlier decision.'

A smile broke out across Dana's face. 'Oh, thank you,' she breathed. Suddenly her elation disappeared.

'Oh, my gosh. Lisa's wedding cake has to be decorated by Saturday.'

'Sorry, but you won't be doing much for the next two weeks, give or take a few days.'

'You're kidding.' Horror crossed Dana's face. 'I have to get that cake ready. I can't lose the money.'

'You don't have a choice,' Naomi said gently. She was about to recommend notifying the hospital social worker to thrust the problem into his or her lap when Lacey interrupted.

'Don't worry about the cake. I'll call some of the other women who have a decorating business. As for Allie and Catrina, we'll work something out whether Dr Stewart keeps you here or sends you home. I know several ladies from our church who'd be happy to watch the girls.'

'I hate to bother anyone.'

'It's no bother,' Lacey insisted. 'Just leave it to me.'

Naomi stared at the nurse. She wasn't used to dealing with family problems; she usually wrote out a referral to one of Lakeside's social workers. They handled the personal details and the medical staff didn't get involved beyond acting as a consultant if questions arose about the patient's care.

Over the next few hours Naomi was pleasantly surprised by the response of the locals. In what seemed like the blink of an eye, someone had organized a schedule of caretakers and meal deliveries. An older couple agreed to drive Dana home and pick up her children from the day care center.

There didn't seem to be any real strangers in Deer Creek since everyone gave their assistance willingly, some offering without being asked. The generosity exhibited tugged at Naomi's heartstrings.

It was awesome.

By the time her familiar weariness descended it was time for Dana's final assessment. Thank goodness the end of her shift was near.

She squared her shoulders and strode into Dana's cubicle to re-examine her hands. 'The burns don't appear any worse than they did earlier,' she announced after several long moments. 'Quick showering made all the difference.'

'Then I can go home?' Dana asked, her voice eager, her hazel eyes alight with anticipation.

Naomi smiled. 'I suppose. Who's your family physician?'

'Dr Parker.'

The familiar name made Naomi pause. Hopefully, he'd concur with her decision not to hospitalize the young mother. 'It's important for someone to watch for complications so be sure that he sees you tomorrow. If he can't work you into his schedule, come here.'

'I will.'

'I'll apply an antibiotic and a bulky dressing on your hands before we release you,' Naomi said. 'Your legs shouldn't need anything more than a skin moisturizer. Are you allergic to any medication or had a recent tetanus injection?'

Dana shook her head.

'I want you to take penicillin four times a day for a few days and Lacey will give you a tetanus booster before you leave. I can also prescribe codeine for the pain or, if you prefer, you can use aspirin.'

'I'd rather take the over-the-counter medicine,' Dana said. 'It's been working so far.'

'OK, but if you need something stronger call me. There's no point in suffering.'

A short time later, with her hands dressed and splinted and wearing a borrowed scrub suit as the acid had eaten holes in her uniform, Dana left.

With her departure, the steady stream of people who'd come to help the single mother dried up and the emergency room became deathly quiet once again.

Naomi took time to reflect on the case. She couldn't believe that she hadn't admitted Dana and given her over into Adam's care, but she was glad she hadn't. Should Adam question her decision, she already had her defense planned.

Taking advantage of the inactivity, Naomi found a private spot in the doctors' lounge and telephoned Dr Davenport. Lakeside's physician was easier to reach than she'd predicted but, although she eloquently explained how she was ready to resume her usual duties, he wouldn't be dissuaded.

'I don't intend to upset the status quo now,' he told her. 'Naturally, I don't want to compromise Deer Creek's ER coverage but if your skills can be better utilized elsewhere, especially to help an old friend, I won't stand in the way. Don't overwork yourself, but do whatever it takes to make the plan work and Parker happy.'

With a grimace and a sigh of resignation, she broke the connection and returned to her unit.

Irritated by her failure, Naomi indulged herself with a soft drink. She'd popped the top of an aluminum grape soda can when a tall, bony woman in her mid-sixties stormed through the double doors.

She wore a heather-gray skirt and a pink blouse with

a cameo at her throat. Her matching gray jacket bore a hospital name tag on the right lapel and she clutched several cream-colored manila folders to her chest.

Fascinated by the grim determination on the unknown woman's thin face and the out-of-date bouffant hair-style, Naomi tried to recall if she'd been introduced to this person. No, she hadn't, she decided. She'd have remembered this unforgettable individual.

'Aunt Rachel! What brings you here?' Lacey flashed Naomi a warning glance before she smiled at the silver-haired visitor.

Rachel Parker. The head of Medical Records. Naomi mentally thanked Lacey for the cue.

Rachel approached on soft-soled shoes, reminiscent of those belonging to the first librarian Naomi had ever known. The tight lines around her pinched mouth soft-ened as she stared at her niece and placed the folders on the counter. 'Work, as usual.'

She turned her steely gaze on Naomi. 'Dr Stewart, I presume?'

'Yes.' Naomi rose and extended her hand. 'It's a pleasure to meet you at last.'

Rachel blinked, as if surprised by Naomi's greeting. She laid one pale hand in Naomi's before pulling it away. 'Yes, well, I understand my subordinate gave you the orientation to our medical records system in my absence,' she said in a businesslike tone.

Naomi felt a sudden surge of sympathy for the girl she'd met in Rachel's stead. Rachel Parker obviously wasn't an easy woman to work for. 'She did an excellent job.'

'I beg to differ. If she had, I wouldn't be here now,' Rachel replied. She raised the reading glasses which hung from her neck on a gold chain and perched them on her nose, before opening the top folder.

'Your records concerning Chester Lang's treatment are incomplete.'

'That's impossible.'

Rachel peered at Naomi over her spectacles. 'Patient records are my business. I know what I'm talking about.'

So do I, Naomi wanted to say, but she restrained herself. 'What's missing?'

'The treatment notes and the discharge summary. You didn't fill out a death certificate either.' Before Naomi could protest Rachel flipped the second folder open. 'As you can see, the physician orders section in Kevin Warner's chart only contains your notation to transfer him to Lakeside.'

Naomi couldn't believe the pages in front of her. Detailed record-keeping was a must and a task she prided herself on performing both accurately and in a timely way. 'Something is wrong.'

'I'd say so.' Rachel's voice was sharp. 'You may be able to get by at Lakeside with poor documentation practices but you won't here.'

'The error isn't on my part. I distinctly remember completing my paperwork. The pieces are either mis-filed or misplaced.'

'That has to be it,' Lacey said. 'I saw Dr Stewart writing in the charts myself. I also made copies to send along with Mr Warner when he was transferred.'

Naomi felt a measure of relief. If Rachel didn't believe her at least she'd believe Lacey. 'Perhaps you should review the other files you received that day.'

Suggesting a review opened a door to Naomi's

memory. Like a slow-motion replay, she saw Adam Parker as he'd stood over her in the ER, vocalizing his intention to read Chester Lang's chart. Had he followed through with his plan? And, if so, would he deliberately sabotage documents to discredit her?

No, she decided. Adam Parker might be gruff but he wasn't the type to deliberately undermine another physician. The missing pages posed a simple clerical problem. They'd turn up eventually—they *had* to.

But if the problem was more serious and if Adam wasn't involved then who was?

Naomi vowed to be on the alert: she couldn't afford any bad reports filtering back to Dr Davenport when her future was at stake.

Rachel tapped the pages until all the edges were perfectly flush with each other before the she closed the folders. 'As part of our quality assurance protocol, I'll have to notify my nephew.'

'By all means.' Naomi refused to bow down to the older woman's intimidation tactics. 'Do whatever you think is right.'

Rachel's jaw dropped as if she'd expected a fight and was disappointed that her wish hadn't been granted. Finally her mouth closed with a snap. 'Hmm,' she said, gathering the files to her chest and pivoting away as sharply as a cadet on a parade maneuver.

Lacey waited until the double doors swung closed and they were alone once again. 'There goes a frustrated woman.'

Naomi held her counsel.

'She never married and she always doted on Grandpa. Aunt Rachel has never worked anywhere else but here.

This job is her whole life.' Lacey grinned. 'I'm sure you could tell that.'

Naomi's smile was rueful. 'Maybe she needs a hobby.'

'We've suggested it, but she says she's too busy. Goosebumps run down my spine when I imagine what life will be like for us once she retires. She only has a few years until then.'

'Send her on a cruise. Maybe she'll meet someone.'

Lacey snapped her fingers. 'I never thought of that. What a wonderful idea.'

'Speaking of wonderful ideas, I'm calling it quits for today.'

'Lucky you,' Lacey said. 'I'm on until eight. By the way, you are coming to the annual hospital picnic tomorrow night, aren't you?'

Naomi shrugged off the white lab coat with her name personalized in maroon letters, and hung it on a wall peg behind the desk. 'I don't have a choice, do I?'

'Not really. Hey, how about a movie? There's a new one playing. An adventure.'

Naomi stifled a yawn. 'The only thing I want to see for the next few hours is the back of my eyelids.' She winked at Lacey. 'You could ask Dale. I hear he's off today.'

Lacey colored a bright shade of pink. 'Maybe I will. You know, we could see the late show. Make it a foursome.'

'You two, me and who else?'

'Adam. It would do both of you some good to relax around each other.'

'It probably would but it won't happen.' Naomi

grabbed her purse from the bottom drawer of the desk. 'See you tomorrow.'

An hour later, clad in a gray sleeveless pullover and a pair of matching shorts, she sank into a lounge chair on Hank's back-yard deck. Warmed by the sun and lulled by the sounds of birds chirping, leaves rustling and water sprinkling like raindrops, she relaxed.

She loved this time of day. Hank did, too, and whenever patients didn't demand his time they'd pass the hours together. Although she hadn't anticipated forming a deep friendship with anyone during her few months in Deer Creek, she'd already grown fond of him. His easygoing ways and non-judgemental attitude made it understandable why everyone in the community held him in high regard.

The two squirrels Hank had named Lester and Lizzie scampered over the branches of the huge oak tree in one corner of the property, scolding each other at one point. Shortly afterwards, their differences apparently resolved, the two resumed their playful antics.

Accustomed to confronting issues head-on, she decided to handle the uncomfortable situation with Adam Parker in the same straightforward manner. Whatever barriers stood between them had to come down—it was the only way they could work together.

As for her own fears of getting too attached to the locals, this stint in general practice was only temporary.

Adam glanced at his watch before pressing the doorbell several times in rapid succession. He'd gone looking for Hank since no one had been able to reach him by telephone or seen him for several hours. Although

Hank's Mercedes was parked in the driveway next to Naomi's Mustang, Adam didn't see any signs of activity.

Considering how Hank had seemed slower and more preoccupied than usual today, Adam was concerned.

This time he tried the doorknob. It turned and he pushed his way inside.

The interior was cool and dark and strangely quiet. He wandered down the hallway, peering into the main rooms as he worked his way to the back of the house. 'Hank? Naomi?'

He bypassed the stairs, intending to search this level first. The kitchen was in its usual pristine condition so the small scrap of paper on the table caught his eye.

'Went golfing,' it read. Recognizing Hank's handwriting, Adam relaxed. He should have known—Hank always golfed with a few of his cronies on Wednesday afternoons. His concern over his partner was making his imagination run wild. It was time he forced Hank to give him some answers, and if Hank didn't have any then Adam would personally check him into the hospital for a complete physical.

Turning to leave, he glanced through the patio doors into the backyard and froze in his tracks.

Naomi was curled in a deck chair.

No wonder she hadn't heard the doorbell. He debated leaving unnoticed, then decided that this was the perfect opportunity to learn if she'd called Davenport.

His loafers made soft thuds against the linoleum floor and the heavy glass door slid to the right with a muted rumble. A noisy cardinal hopped across the freshly mown lawn and the neighbor's Great Dane barked at the calico cat walking along the top of the wooden fence separating the property.

He moved to the chair opposite hers, her bare feet and long legs coming into his line of vision first as he approached. True, the sight was a common one as it was summertime and he'd grown up in a household of women but, nonetheless, he found it disconcerting.

Naomi wasn't his sister and his body knew it.

He skirted the furniture, noticing her closed eyes. From the sliver of ice in her water glass and the lack of condensation, she'd been outside for some time.

The chair cushion whispered softly as he sat in Hank's favorite seat and waited for her reaction to the noise. She didn't stir.

Leaning back to observe her, he placed his elbows on the arm rests and clasped his hands together.

Her gray shorts had a small rip near one hem and her shirt had a red paint splotch on one shoulder. The obviously old and well-worn outfit seemed out of character for an aspiring shift supervisor candidate.

His gaze traveled upward. Her chest rose and fell almost imperceptibly and occasionally he heard a small sigh, accompanied by a smile. Was she dreaming of a former lover? Unhappy with the idea, he frowned.

Her shoulder blades seemed more prominent, her cheek-bones and the dark smudges under her eyes more pronounced. Had she lost weight? Not in the days since she'd arrived but in recent weeks?

The breeze ruffled the newspaper in her lap and a large bottle skidded across the redwood deck. Its contents rattled with the characteristic sound of pills tumbling against each other.

Adam retrieved the bottle as it rolled in his direction.

High-potency vitamins. Prescription strength.

Several things which had puzzled him snapped into place. He carefully placed the vial on the small table next to her cup.

Her wristwatch beeped. She sighed and her eyelids fluttered open. With a sudden intake of breath, she jumped. 'Adam!'

'I didn't mean to scare you,' he said.

'No problem,' she said, yawning. 'If you're looking for Hank he's not here.'

As she unfolded her long, slender legs his imagination shifted into overdrive. He cleared his throat. 'I know. I saw the note. I was concerned about him, but it appears I should be concerned about you.'

A furrow appeared across her forehead. 'What makes you say that?'

He pointed to the plastic cylinder on the table. 'You're ill, aren't you?'

CHAPTER FIVE

NAOMI squirmed under Adam's intent gaze and struggled to break through the few fingers of fog still clouding her brain. 'What makes you say that?'

Adam gave her a long-suffering look. 'Healthy young women don't usually sleep soundly in the middle of the day, look pale and exhausted all the time or take prescription vitamins.'

'There's a logical explanation,' she began.

'There always is.' His eyes grew wide. 'I might have known. You're pregnant!'

The idea was so inconceivable that she could only stare at him blankly.

He ran his hand over his head. 'This won't work. We've been pushing abstinence in our schools for years. Having an unwed *physician*, no less, will create—'

Naomi burst out laughing. 'I hope you don't always make such snap diagnoses, Doctor, because the one you just made is horribly flawed.'

'Is it?'

She smiled. 'Absolutely.' Although he didn't appear convinced, she didn't feel it necessary to explain the reasons in detail. As a goal-oriented student, she'd ranked sexual experimentation way down on her list of priorities. Her virginity was no one's business but her own, the as-yet-unknown man in her life and her personal physician. Since Adam didn't fall in any of those categories she saw no reason to enlighten him.

'I had infectious mononucleosis this past spring,' she said, hating to divulge the information. Yet, as her temporary partner, he deserved to know.

'Unfortunately, I'm one of the lucky one to two per cent of people who suffer from chronic fatigue after an Epstein-Barr virus infection.'

She shrugged before continuing. 'I couldn't keep up with the pace at Lakeside so—'

'Davenport sent you here to recuperate,' he finished.

'Afraid so.'

'Any other complications?'

She shook her head. 'None.'

'Does Hank know?'

'Yes.'

He pinched the bridge of his nose, obviously at a loss over the new development. In the ensuing silence a cardinal called to his mate. Finally Adam straightened. 'This really throws a kink in things.'

'It shouldn't. I'm fully capable of performing my job and Hank's at the same time.' She added her final argument. 'If Hank didn't think I could handle a small portion of his patient load he wouldn't have suggested it.'

'I need someone I can count on. I don't want to worry that you'll collapse on me or on someone in ER.'

Since the very scenario he'd mentioned had actually happened to her, Naomi felt her skin warm. Hopefully he'd attribute her rising color to the heat and not to his accusation hitting home.

'I won't.'

His face took on a pained expression. 'If it weren't for Hank I wouldn't agree to this.'

She met his gaze, mentally applauding a man who

consented to participate in a distasteful situation for the sake of a friend. 'I know. For the record, neither would I.'

'Then why are you?'

If only she understood the reasons herself. 'I'm not sure. Maybe because he sees me for what I am. Maybe because he's a generous man. Maybe I'm losing my mind. Regardless, my assistance is only temporary.' At his quizzical look she added, 'Until you find someone who wants to take over part of Hank's practice.'

His features relaxed. 'Oh, yeah.' He rose and, after taking two steps toward the sliding glass door, stopped. 'When do you want to start?'

'Anytime.'

'It'll take a few days to clear it with our hospital administration. Shall we say next Monday?'

'No problem.'

He took another step before pausing. 'Has Hank talked to you?'

Reading between the proverbial lines, it seemed safer to pretend ignorance. 'About what?'

He raised one eyebrow. 'How bad is he?'

She answered honestly. 'I don't know.'

'Then he *does* have a medical problem?'

'I didn't say that. Even if I knew his condition I couldn't tell you. These are questions you should be asking him.'

He nodded once. 'By the way, I talked to Chester Lang's wife.'

She tensed.

'Sabrina suspected he was gone before the ambulance arrived. I apologize for placing the blame on you.'

'Accepted. Did you read the chart, too?'

'No. Should I?'

She shrugged. 'I understand some of my notes are missing. I wondered when and where they might have gone.'

'Aunt Rachel will find them,' he advised, appearing unconcerned. 'She can find anything that's been mis-filed. She's like a bloodhound when it comes to patient records.'

He slid the door closed, leaving her alone once again. Where before the solitude had felt comforting, now it seemed lonely.

She settled back into the chair to watch the squirrels and reflect on Adam's attitude toward her. Although they had not formally called a truce, she sensed that they had reached one.

All because of Hank, she thought, although Chester Lang's wife had probably factored into it as well. Regardless of how or why, she was glad to establish peace.

As for Adam wondering why she'd agreed to help Hank, she didn't want to voice her real reasons.

She wanted a taste of what Adam had.

'I wan' my momma.' Four-year-old Tina Newsome screamed her dismay while Naomi examined the radius of her left arm.

'Momma's at home,' Mr Newsome patiently explained as he held his daughter in his lap. 'We'll see her soon.'

'Wanna see her *now*,' Tina howled.

'We'll get some X-rays,' Naomi said. 'To be honest, I'll be surprised if her arm isn't broken.'

'She fell off the jungle gym pretty hard. I suppose

it's only to be expected.' He sighed. 'She's such a daredevil; it's hard to keep up with her.'

'Daddy, my arm hurts.' Tina's rosebud mouth trembled and tears trickled down her dusty face.

Naomi bent down to speak at Tina's level. 'I know, sweetie. We're going to take a few special pictures before we can fix it.'

The little girl shook her head so hard that her pigtails slapped her father's face. 'Don' wan' no pitchers.'

'Tina, stop it,' he warned.

Naomi dug in her lab coat pocket and retrieved her shiny fifty-cent piece. 'Do you see this, Tina?'

The child nodded, momentarily distracted.

With a quick move, Naomi made the silver coin disappear. The child's eyes grew wide. 'Where'd it go?'

'I don't know.' Naomi pretended surprise. 'Oh, look, I see it.' She leaned closer to the child and reached for her ear. 'Is this it?'

Tina giggled. 'How'd it get there?'

'Magic.'

'Do it again,' she demanded.

'After we take the special pictures,' Naomi said.

Appeased by the promise, Tina went with Lacey to Radiology for the X-rays. Before long they returned and a technician brought the films for Naomi to examine.

'Magic,' Tina demanded in the forthright manner of children, and Naomi smiled as she dug in her pocket.

Once again, after exhibiting the coin, it disappeared. Tina's eyes sparkled with interest. 'Where is it?' she asked, glancing all around.

Naomi placed a finger on her cheek-bone and pretended to be puzzled. 'I'm not sure. Oh, wait a minute.

What's this?' She lifted one pigtail. 'Here it is,' she said, withdrawing the coin.

'Oh,' Tina breathed.

'Will you hold this for me?' At Tina's nod, Naomi pressed the money into her hand. 'Don't lose it or we can't make any more magic.'

Tina shook her head and sat down. 'Won't.'

With her small patient momentarily satisfied, Naomi stuffed the films onto the viewbox and flipped the switch. Tina's bones appeared opaque against the dark background.

Naomi pointed to a dark, transverse line midway between the wrist and elbow. 'There's the fracture. We'll splint it,' she told Lacey in a low voice. Immediately, Lacey began assembling the necessary supplies.

'She won't like wearing a cast,' Mr Newsome warned.

'She doesn't have a choice.' Naomi bent down. 'Tina? I'm going to put something hard on your arm to hold it in place so the broken bone can heal. It's called a cast.'

Tina stared at her. 'Will it hurt?'

'No. It will make your arm feel better.'

'OK.'

Lacey showed Tina the various packages of casting material in a brilliant array of colors. 'Which color would you like?'

Tina pointed to the fluorescent pink. 'Good choice. That's my favorite too,' Lacey said.

While Lacey soaked the plaster bandage Naomi applied a layer of sheet wadding and a stockinette over Tina's arm. Next she wrapped the wet bandage around

Tina's hand, keeping the child's wrist and elbow joints flexed to lessen any stiffness.

Naomi worked quickly before the plaster dried, monitoring Tina's fingers for any loss of movement or changes in the skin's appearance. As she finished she carefully secured the stockinette over the raw edges.

Lacey adjusted a pediatric sling to fit Tina's frame while Naomi gave Mr Newsome the care instructions. 'Keep the cast dry. She'll also complain of itching but don't let her poke anything into the cast to scratch it. Her arm may be painful for a few days, but if it lasts longer than that see your doctor.'

'How long will she need to wear it?'

'About eight weeks. Your physician will take X-rays first to be sure the bone's healed. Use pillows to elevate her arm while she's sleeping—she'll be more comfortable. I know it's hot and the sling will bother her but she needs the support it provides.'

Naomi felt a tug on her jacket sleeve and she looked down.

Tina opened her palm to reveal the silver coin. 'Can I see your magic once more 'fore I go?' she begged. 'Ple-e-e-ease?'

Naomi chuckled at the little girl's expression. How could she resist such a plea? She glanced at Mr Newsome, catching his slight nod and the benevolent smile he bestowed on his daughter. Tina was obviously accustomed to having her wishes granted.

She gave in. 'OK.'

A sunny smile lit up Tina's face. 'Goody!'

Naomi took the coin, noticing that she had Lacey's and Mr Newsome's attention as well. With a twist of her wrist the money vanished. 'Where did it go?' she asked Tina.

Tina hopped on one foot, then the other. 'Show me. Show me.'

Naomi touched the fingers of Tina's casted arm and slowly withdrew the fifty-cent piece out of the sling.

Tina stared up at her father. 'Do it, too, Daddy.'

'Sorry, hon. I don't know how.' Mr Newsome shook Naomi's hand. 'Thank you, Dr Stewart. For everything.'

'My pleasure.'

Father and daughter left, leaving Lacey and Naomi to straighten the room for the next casualty.

'You're a woman of many talents,' Lacey said. 'I'm impressed. Next thing you'll be on the road with an act. Like David Copperfield.'

Naomi laughed. 'Since it's the only magic trick in my bag, I don't think Mr Copperfield has to worry. It took me years to get the technique right.'

'What technique?' a tenor voice asked.

Startled, Naomi glanced toward the doorway and saw Adam framed in the opening. The utterly masculine picture he presented caused her throat to go dry and the sentence she was about to say went unspoken.

It was ridiculous for his presence to unnerve her so— after fighting her way in a male-dominated profession the sight of Adam Parker shouldn't affect her at all. There was absolutely no reason why a glimpse of him should drive home the differences between men and women.

Unfortunately it did. So far she hadn't found the antidote to counteract this strange affliction.

'Oh, nothing. Just something I learned as a kid that occasionally comes in handy with the younger crowd.'

Naomi changed the subject. 'Did you need something?'

He shook his head as he moved closer toward them. 'Just delivering a message. The administrator and the medical staff approved our revised emergency room coverage.'

Naomi stared at him in surprise. 'How did you manage that? We only decided last night.'

'I laid the groundwork the other day,' he admitted. 'After you agreed I called a meeting to make the formal decision. We'll begin the new schedule next week.'

Lacey glanced at Adam, then Naomi. 'What's going on?'

'Hank's decided to slow down so Naomi is easing into the practice. She'll see patients in our office two days a week.'

Lacey's face lit up like a firework display. 'Then you're staying? That's wonderful.'

'Oh, no,' Naomi corrected her. 'This arrangement is only until Adam finds someone to take over on a permanent basis.'

'Oh.' Lacey's disappointment was obvious.

'Dr Stewart has her own career plans,' Adam said. 'We can't expect her to change them for us.' Naomi detected a faint note of derision in his voice and her hackles rose. Surely he wasn't one of those men who were intimidated by sharing their chosen field with a woman.

Impossible, she decided. He was too self-assured to hold such an antiquated opinion. It had to be something else.

Lacey scoffed. 'Plans are made to be changed.'

'Now that's a philosophical statement,' Adam said.

'If you're going to spout clichés get them right. It's "rules are made to be broken".'

Naomi felt a need to become part of the conversation rather than be the subject. 'Regardless, I have a life in Kansas City.'

'Yeah, right.' Lacey rolled her eyes upward. 'With no family or friends, what's there for you? Besides the hospital, that is?'

Nothing, Naomi almost said, but stopped herself. She'd been striving to attain her goal of success ever since her youth. Now that it lay within her grasp she refused to let it slip through her fingers. 'My work at Lakeside is very fulfilling.'

Lacey opened her mouth but Adam forestalled her. 'Dr Stewart knows what she wants. Nothing you say will change her mind.' Once again his voice possessed a hard edge and she wondered at the cause.

'She's not like Cynthia—'

'Lace,' he warned, his jaw squared. 'Don't you have something to do? Preferably in another room?'

Lacey flounced to the door. 'I'm going. But you're right—I won't change her mind. Maybe if you gave her the proper incentive she would.' With that, she stormed from the cubicle.

The silence was so complete that Naomi could have heard a suture needle drop. Adam obviously had incendiary feelings for this Cynthia if the mere mention of her name caused him to close himself off.

'I apologize for my sister's emotional outburst,' he said stiffly.

'She expressed her feelings and opinions. You can't fault her for that. I'm curious, though. Do you have something against women with a career?'

'Not at all.'

'Then why—?'

He cut her off. 'My former fiancée, Cynthia St John, was—is—a physician. An extremely goal-oriented one.'

The words 'like you' hung in the air and Naomi was sorry she'd brought up the subject.

'We'd planned to share our practice but she didn't like the idea of spending her days here. She loved the big city, especially Washington, D.C. After she took a trip there she referred to us as 'the little D.C.' and it was always in a condescending manner. It wasn't surprising to anyone, myself included, when she moved to the D.C. she loved.'

Naomi touched his forearm, feeling the warmth of his bare skin. Now she understood why he'd always seemed to withdraw whenever her temporary status was mentioned. 'I'm sorry.'

'Now you know the whole sordid story.'

'If it means anything, I think she made the wrong choice.'

He studied her for a moment. 'What would you do if you were in the same situation?'

The idea was bitter-sweet. 'I'd like to think I wouldn't turn my back on the man I loved, but there are a lot of variables to consider.' She forced a smile. 'Since I'm not in that predicament it's a moot point.'

'You're right. It is.' He turned to go.

'Adam?' she asked impulsively.

He stopped. 'Yes?'

'Will you be at the picnic tonight?'

One corner of his mouth turned upward. 'The

founding father's grandson not be there? I'd never be forgiven.' He paused. 'I'll save you a seat.'

The seat Adam had saved was actually a spot on a patchwork denim quilt that had obviously been used on numerous occasions in its lifetime.

Carrying a paper plate which held a barbecued hot dog, a dollop of potato salad and a spoonful of baked beans, Lacey plopped down next to Naomi. 'Has Mom regaled you with the story of our picnic blanket yet?'

Naomi glanced at the matriarch of the Parker clan. Unlike her son, Rosie Parker was of average height, twenty pounds overweight and wore a perpetual smile on her round face. 'No, afraid not.'

'Golly. You're slipping, Mom,' Lacey teased her mother.

'Nonsense. I was simply waiting for the right time.' Rosie smiled at her daughter. 'But you go ahead, dear.'

While Naomi drank her fruit punch Lacey began pointing out the various blocks. 'Mom saved all of our worn-out jeans. None of us understood why until she started this project.'

She pointed to several faded squares. 'Those came from a pair of mine that I split when I was crawling under Grandpa's fence. The pinstripe was Melissa's and this stripe was from one of my farmer grandad's overalls. To add color, she threw in squares of fabric from other outfits—like our first prom dresses. Everyone in the family is represented here—even Hank.'

Naomi touched a piece of cowboy-and-Indian flannel. 'Was this Adam's?'

Lacey grinned. 'His pajamas, in fact. We have a

picture of him wearing them. He was eight and looked scrawny, but cute.'

'No kidding?' Without thinking, Naomi glanced over at Adam who was standing a few feet away, talking with several people she recognized from the hospital.

Surprisingly enough, he hadn't dressed with a formality befitting his status in the hospital hierarchy. He wore a pair of tan shorts and a black short-sleeved rugby-style shirt. With his muscular legs braced apart and his arms folded across his chest, he looked daring and dangerous—and totally in control.

The scrawny body of an eight-year-old boy had matured to a level exceeding many women's expectations, including her own. She'd bet money that he didn't sleep in or even own a pair of pajamas.

Naomi pulled her thoughts out of the bedroom as Lacey ended her recitation. 'You've done a marvelous job, Mrs Parker,' Naomi said, tracing the outline of one square.

Mrs Parker smiled. 'Thank you. And please call me Rosie. Everyone does. By the way, Lacey, where's Dale?'

Lacey's face turned pink. 'He's working but he'll be along later.' She stared into the distance. 'Here comes the rest of our family.'

The twins, Evelyn and Melissa, approached along with the youngest sister, Amy. The three women's resemblance to their older brother was uncanny. They were tall and slender and Naomi felt like a plain Jane surrounded by beauty contestants. Although they stared at Naomi with undisguised speculation during the introductions, they welcomed her with sincerity.

Naomi felt at home with them, which was surprising

in itself. It must be the relaxed atmosphere, she decided.

'We're a lot younger than Adam, in case you didn't notice,' Evelyn said.

'I wondered.'

'Adam was born nine months to the day after his father and I were married,' Rosie said with a smile. 'With his dad in medical school it was a struggle so we waited to add to our family. We almost waited too long, though. Lacey arrived ten years later. The twins came eleven months after she did and Amy followed three years after that.'

'Last, but not least,' Amy joked.

'Yeah, well, have you broken your news to Adam yet?' Melissa asked, brushing her manicured hands together before she flicked a blade of grass off her name-brand shorts.

Amy's blonde curls bounced as she shook her head. 'I'm waiting to soften him up first.'

'Better ask him in a public place,' Evelyn advised. 'He won't argue so much.'

'What won't I argue about?' Adam asked as he reached the edge of their circle.

Amy glowered at her sister. 'I've been accepted on my first choice master's degree program.'

'That's great.' Adam glanced around. 'Where's Hank?'

'He's pitching horseshoes,' Evelyn answered.

Adam glanced in the direction of the horseshoe pit. 'Where does a person get a degree in medieval history? New York? Philadelphia?'

'A little farther east,' Melissa muttered.

His brow furrowed as he contemplated the geography.

'Europe,' Amy said. 'England, to be exact.'

'Good heavens!' he exploded. 'Couldn't you find a university in the States?'

'Yeah, but where's a better place to learn than in a country steeped in history?' Amy said. 'Just think of the old documents, the castles, the graveyards. They go back hundreds and hundreds of years.'

He shook his head. 'Out of the question. The cost would be enormous. How do you propose to pay for this?'

'I've got a job; I'm saving my money. Besides, George wants to go along. We'll share living expenses.'

'Absolutely not. George is a leech and if he goes you can't.'

'I'm twenty-four years old, Adam. I don't need your permission.'

Naomi recognized that she didn't belong in the family discussion but didn't know how to extricate herself. In the end, keeping a low profile seemed more expedient.

'For heaven's sake, Adam. Amy's old enough to stand on her own two feet and make her own decisions,' Evelyn said. 'Naomi's a woman of the world. She agrees with us, don't you?'

All pairs of eyes turned on her, but the only ones she noticed were Adam's. He raised one sardonic eyebrow.

Naomi gulped. Caught between a rock and a hard place. 'It's not my place to say—'

'Please?' Amy interjected.

'—but studying in England would be a once-in-a-lifetime experience,' Naomi finished, keeping her attention on Adam's handsome face.

'Add her to the family,' Evelyn ordered. 'She's one of us.'

Embarrassed by the attention and Adam's piercing gaze, Naomi's face warmed. Luckily he didn't comment.

'Amy is an adult,' he agreed, 'but, considering who will foot most of the cost, she needs my consent. And my signature. If George is going then she's not.'

'What if George doesn't go?' Amy persisted.

Naomi had the uncanny feeling that the youngest Parker had rigged the conversation. She steeled her face to hide her grin, wondering if Adam had realized it.

He looked thoughtful. 'I know a few people in London,' he said. 'If you agree to check in with them from time to time I suppose it would be all right.'

Amy squealed. She ran over to her brother and flung her arms around his neck. 'This is wonderful. Oh, I can't wait.'

'I'm sure you can't,' he said, wryly.

Naomi hugged her knees to her chest. A totally illogical desire to throw her own arms around Adam's chest came over her. She wondered if his broad shoulders felt as hard and strong as they looked.

Amy stepped back as quickly as she'd descended upon Adam. 'Bye, guys.' With a jaunty wave she was off, presumably to tell her friends of the boon she'd been granted.

Adam moved to Naomi's side. Towering over her, he held out his hand. She stared at it first in surprise, then looked up at his face, certain that a lecture on minding her own business was forthcoming.

His smile appeared genuine and she relaxed. 'If you'll excuse us,' he told the group, 'Naomi and I need to mingle.'

She placed her hand in his palm and rose with his

assistance. The feeling of his fingers closing over hers sent a shiver down her spine, and she felt oddly bereft when he broke the contact.

'You're not leaving until Naomi tells me what her perfume is called,' Melissa declared. 'It's fabulous.'

'I'm not sure,' Naomi admitted. 'It's one of those new designer-copy fragrances.'

'Really?' Lacey stared at her brother as if she found the fact interesting and thought that he would, too. 'Where do you buy it?'

'Discount stores carry it. I'll look at the label when I get home and let you know the name.'

'Please do,' Melissa said.

'Visit anytime,' Rosie added. 'You're always welcome.'

'Thanks.' Naomi smiled, certain that she'd never take her up on the offer. As she and Adam ambled away she said, 'Your family is wonderful.'

'I agree.' He grinned. 'I enjoy playing devil's advocate whenever my sisters want something. They usually come up with interesting strategies in an effort to gain my approval.'

Naomi stopped to stare at him. 'Then you knew?'

He paused. 'Of course. They do it all the time.'

'Then why didn't you just say yes when Amy first asked to go?'

'Because it was the only way she would agree to let some of my British friends keep an eye on her.'

Naomi shook her head. 'You really are sneaky, aren't you?'

He shrugged. 'Being the only male in a household of females has a tendency to foster the trait. Besides, someone has to keep their feet on the ground. If anything happened to them because of their impulsiveness when I could have stopped it. . .' His voice died. 'Besides, Mom doesn't need the grief they'd give her.'

'I understand,' she said. And she did. Adam was a protector by nature, and she wondered if his sisters realized or appreciated this trait.

They walked on, stopping to talk to hospital employees from all departments and ranks. He had a flair for knowing what to discuss with each person. Once again Naomi was reminded of a feudal lord, surveying his underlings, although he possessed a knack for making them feel equal.

Occasionally she noted a few envious glances from women and glowed with female satisfaction at having him act as her escort.

Adam wasn't hers, and never would be, but for the moment it was exciting to pretend.

Eventually he guided her toward the refreshment table. 'Enough mingling. How about a drink before we head over to the horseshoe pit and see how the game is going?'

'I'm ready.'

He filled two large paper cups with iced tea out of the insulated containers and handed one to her.

Just as she raised the cup to her mouth Melissa came running toward them. Her long hair was tangled and her breath came out in short spurts as if she'd been in a race.

'You have to come, Adam.'

He tensed. His congenial smile disappeared, replaced by concern. 'Is it Mom?'

She shook her head. 'It's Hank. He's collapsed.'

CHAPTER SIX

DISMAYED by Melissa's announcement, Naomi's heart leaped into her throat. Not Hank. Not now that she'd become attached to him.

'Where?' Adam demanded, looking like a jungle cat ready to spring into action.

'Over by the horseshoes.'

'Let's go,' he said, tossing his paper cup toward the fifty-five-gallon drum being used as a trash receptacle. Naomi did the same, running to keep up with his frantic pace.

They dodged a few clusters of people until word spread and the sea of people parted out of their way.

By the time they had travelled across the picnic grounds a crowd had assembled near the horseshoes, and Naomi's skin glistened with perspiration.

In the center of the commotion Naomi and Adam found Lacey cradling Hank's head in her lap. Naomi was relieved to find the older man conscious.

The worry lines on Adam's face smoothed out. 'What's all this I hear about you making a commotion?' he asked in a lighthearted voice to mask his concern.

Hank lifted a hand and waved it weakly in the air. 'It's nothing. Dizzy.'

'His pulse is rapid and he's complaining of muscle cramps,' Lacey reported.

'Any chest pain?' Adam asked.

Hank closed his eyes. 'No. Pain's in my head

and left arm. Nausea, too. Hot. So hot.'

Adam glanced at Naomi. 'Heat exhaustion.'

Since Hank's skin was pale and damp, as opposed to the red and dry appearance of heatstroke victims, Naomi concurred.

She immediately turned to two of the men hovering nearby. 'Can you wet a rag and get us a glass of cool water? Ask around for salt, too.'

'And call an ambulance,' Adam added.

'Right away,' the one man said. Apparently glad of the task—any task, if it would help their beloved Dr Taylor—they disappeared. A moment later someone pressed a cold washcloth into her hand. She passed it to Lacey who dabbed Hank's face while Naomi dumped salt from a shaker into a cup of water.

'Drink this,' she said, pressing the glass to his lips.

Hank took a sip and made a face as he drank the contents. 'Feel ridiculous,' he said.

Adam rubbed at the cramp in Hank's arm. 'You've been neglecting yourself. Now you'll have to slow your wheels.'

'Wanted to finish the game,' Hank muttered.

'Sorry, ace,' Adam said. 'Next time.'

The shrill siren grew louder, then stopped. Rich and Dale jumped from the vehicle, each grabbing a tackle box of supplies and equipment before approaching.

'Transport him,' Naomi ordered. 'You can take his vitals on the way.' Although she was reasonably sure of the diagnosis, other conditions could also have caused his collapse and she hoped to rule those out.

Within minutes the paramedics had loaded Hank into the ambulance and Naomi climbed in behind.

'I'll meet you in ER,' Adam said before he slammed the double doors shut.

Dale pumped up the blood pressure cuff on Hank's arm. 'Wanna bet he'll get there before we do?'

'I wouldn't be surprised,' Naomi said.

However, Adam didn't meet them at the emergency entrance as predicted, and Naomi was glad for the opportunity to have a few private moments with her patient.

'Get the full chemistry profile with electrolytes, along with a blood count,' Naomi ordered once they were inside the cool confines of the trauma room. 'I also want a stat bedside glucose. And don't forget a urine specimen.'

She felt for Hank's pulse, counting the beats. 'Your pulse is still fast. We'll take an EKG just as a precaution.'

Dale and Rich left shortly afterwards, while the nurse on duty made arrangements for the various tests. Before long she returned with the glucose meter, poked Hank's finger and obtained a reading which she showed Naomi.

Naomi glanced at the normal number displayed on the unit. 'Adam's concerned about you.' She spoke in a low voice as she held Hank's hand.

He nodded.

'Will you tell him what's wrong or do we have to take advantage of your weakened condition and find out for ourselves?'

'I'll tell you.' He sounded resigned. 'Not now, though. When you're together.'

A moment later the lab technicians appeared—one to fix the heart leads to his chest and the other to draw the requested blood samples.

'Time for another drink,' Naomi said, sticking a straw in the salty water she'd prepared. After he'd finished she patted his arm. 'Just rest.'

She walked into the hallway and met Adam, looking harried. 'How is he?' he asked hoarsely.

'He's doing fine. We don't have the test results back yet but he's resting.'

He motioned to the clipboard in her hand. 'May I?'

She handed over her notes, grateful for the courtesy of a request rather than a demand.

Pages rustled as he flipped through the documents. He paused once, raising his head to stare at her with an upraised eyebrow. 'Why the bedside glucose? Is he diabetic?'

'As you can see, the results were within the normal limits.'

Finally, he smoothed the papers flat and handed her the clipboard. 'I want to perform a complete physical. It's probably been years since he's been checked top to bottom.'

Naomi stuck the chart in the crook of one arm. 'Right now *I'm* his doctor.'

'Fine. You do it.'

'Regardless of who does what, we'll wait.' Sensing his growing ire, she tossed out the information which would forestall his argument. 'He wants to talk to you.'

Adam's face became grim. 'I *knew* something was wrong. I should have—'

'Before you jump to conclusions hear what he has to say,' Naomi advised. 'And don't ask me to prepare you because I'm as much in the dark as you are.'

He nodded. Then he squared his shoulders and strode

into the trauma room. 'Well, now, Hank. How's the service?'

Naomi understood the effort it required for Adam to sound relaxed and unconcerned.

'Pretty good, but I still don't recommend it,' Hank said.

Naomi approached the opposite side of the gurney and counted her patient's pulse. 'You're hurting my feelings.'

Adam took Hank's wrinkled hand in his lean one. 'So, what's going on?'

'Oh, Adam.' Hank sighed. 'I knew if I told you you'd worry. You look after so many folks now that I hated to be one more.'

'Nonsense,' Adam replied briskly. 'Regardless of how many friends or family I have, you'll always be at the top of the list.'

Hank smiled and Naomi felt a strange knot form in her throat. She thought back to her own collapse and wondered what it would have been like if someone had *really* been alarmed about her. Davenport had been concerned, but his concern had seemed more superficial.

In that moment she began to see Adam in a different light. He did everything with sincerity and, unexpectedly, her heart stirred with loving emotion.

'I haven't felt perky for some time,' Hank began. 'A virus, I thought. Anyway, when I went to Lakeside to discuss our staffing problem a few weeks ago I had a complete physical.' He motioned for a drink.

Naomi held the cup and guided the straw to his lips, careful to hide the trembling in her hands caused by her new-found awareness.

After Hank had drunk deeply he continued. 'My blood pressure was high and I was anemic. They also found an abdominal aneurysm.'

'An aneurysm?' Adam nearly shouted. 'High blood pressure! And you haven't slowed down?'

'From the sonogram the vascular surgeon didn't feel my case was an emergency. I thought I'd work until my surgery, take my vacation and no one would be the wiser.'

'Were you ever going to tell me?' Adam sounded wounded.

'After everything was over.' Hank's smile was lop-sided. 'Not a good idea, huh?'

'Definitely not.' Adam was adamant. 'I suppose I should be grateful that you collapsed.'

'I was thinking of you,' Hank reminded him.

'And I appreciate your motive, but don't do it again. When is the surgery scheduled?'

'A couple of weeks.'

No wonder he was so anxious for her to step into his shoes, she thought.

'Then you'll have time to relax beforehand,' Adam said. 'Go fishing.'

'But what about my patients?' Hank asked.

Adam gave Naomi a meaningful glance. 'Naomi will take over. I'm sure she can start a few days early.'

'Absolutely. Don't worry about a thing.' Sensing that they needed a moment alone, she said, 'Now, if you'll excuse me, I'm going to check with the lab.'

She returned to the nurses' station just as the remote printer whirred. Slowly one page bearing Henry Taylor's name slid out, then another.

Grabbing them, she scanned the individual sheets.

While his electrolyte results were slightly skewed out of the normal range, they weren't at dangerous levels. Hospitalization wasn't required—only rest, a cool environment and lots of fluids.

She jotted her recommendations onto the proper forms. Just as she finished Adam came around the corner. The slump in his broad shoulders and the weary look in his eyes nearly undid her.

'His lab results are in,' Naomi said. Knowing that Adam wouldn't be satisfied unless he personally reviewed them, she passed the documents to him. 'He can leave any time.'

Adam took a minute to study the numbers. 'I'll bring the car around.'

'I'll tell him.' She skirted the desk but before she took another step Adam stopped her with a hand on her arm.

His warm skin against hers reminded her that she hadn't taken the time to slip a lab coat over the shorts and sleeveless shirt she'd worn to the picnic.

'He's concerned about you.'

She stared at him, incredulous. 'He is? Why?'

'Considering your medical history and your other responsibilities, covering ER along with his practice load may be too much for you.'

'Perhaps,' she answered honestly. 'But if I'm not worrying neither should he.'

He folded his arms across his chest. 'Then you're capable of juggling both positions?'

She met his gaze. 'I get the feeling you're expecting me to let you down.'

His jaw visibly tensed and the truth hit her. 'You are, aren't you?'

His silence was her answer. She gulped back a knot of disappointment. 'Your confidence is awesome.'

'Can you handle it?' he persisted. 'If not, I want to know.'

Naomi straightened her shoulders, determined not to let the hurt he'd caused show. 'I may not have your stamina but, unlike Cynthia and whoever else may have soured your attitude, I won't desert you or let you down. People who know me know that I say what I mean. By the time my three months are up you will, too.'

She marched away, anger adding force to her footsteps. Her eyes burned and her contacts seemed to swim, but she blinked the sensations away. An emotional, teary-eyed individual had no place in medicine—something she'd learned early in her career—and she hated this uncharacteristic weakness rearing its head now.

Without warning, she felt her elbow encased in Adam's steely grip. Before she could extricate herself he'd grabbed her shoulders and turned her round to face him.

'I'm sorry,' he said, his voice rusty, as if apologies didn't come easy.

'You should be.' She tried to move away before the tear she couldn't suppress slipped off her eyelash, but his hold wouldn't lessen.

He tipped her chin upward to stare into her face. His eyes were sorrowful, and without another word he folded her into his embrace.

She buried her nose in his shoulder, reveling in the warmth he exuded, his rock-hard strength and his outdoorsy fragrance tempered with his own inherent masculine scent. For long moments she stood, unable to leave his sheltering arms. Even thoughts of being discovered by a hospital employee didn't spur her into action.

He stroked her hair, entwining some of the loose strands back into her braid. 'Better?'

She nodded, then slowly pulled away.

Once again he tipped her chin upward. This time she saw a different emotion in his eyes—need and want rolled together into something powerful and potent.

Adam lowered his head slowly, methodically, as if allowing her the opportunity to refuse what would come next. But she couldn't. She needed his kiss in the same elemental way she needed air. No other man could possibly meet those requirements.

His mouth descended and she closed her eyes. His firm lips touched hers, first with a feather-light caress and then with demand.

A groan forced its way out of her throat—a sound of longing and of contentment. Her hands snaked around his back and she felt the rippling muscles underneath his shirt.

The intimacy ended abruptly and she felt strangely off-balance. He kept his arm around her, as if he understood that her legs had lost their stiffening.

His breath came in short bursts and her mouth twitched with feminine satisfaction. Obviously this kiss had affected him, too.

'Are you finished?' he asked.

'Finished?' she asked dumbly. 'With what?'

His grin was lopsided. How like a man to take delight in knowing that he'd rendered a woman senseless, she thought, frowning.

'Are you ready to leave?'

Her face warmed at his rephrased question. 'Yes, I am.'

His arms dropped. 'Then I'll drive you two home.'

She nodded. Taking a breath that was more a sigh, she strode into the trauma room.

'I'm releasing you, Hank,' she announced.

He stared at her strangely and her cheeks burned, certain that he'd guessed what had happened in the hallway.

'You two get things worked out?' He glanced first at her, then at Adam.

She studied Adam and nodded.

Adam winked at her, before turning a cheerful face toward his partner. 'To our mutual satisfaction.'

By the end of the next week Naomi felt at home in Adam's practice. It hadn't taken long to learn the office routine, thanks to his capable staff.

Mary, a newly-wed, was Adam's nurse while Lettie assisted Hank, having done so since the early days of his career. Both women were a joy to be around, although Lettie clearly ruled her domain and wasn't afraid to speak her mind.

'I've been telling Dr Taylor that it's time to retire,' Lettie announced on Naomi's first day. 'Maybe now he'll take my advice.' She sniffed. 'Of course he hasn't before so I doubt he will now, the stubborn old goat.'

Naomi had smiled. 'He likes to keep busy.'

'Then he can keep busy with less strenuous activities,' Lettie declared. 'There's all sorts of things he can do to stay active besides spend every waking moment at the office or the hospital.'

'I'm sure he'll find something to do,' Naomi said,

certain that it would be some months before he was well enough to resume even a portion of his practice.

Each evening Naomi went home tired but content. Adam had insisted on taking the late night calls and, although she hadn't argued about it at the time, she vowed that next week would be different. In the meantime, running back and forth between the hospital and Adam's office gave her enough of a load.

It was also interesting to follow up some of the patients she'd treated before. Working strictly in ER didn't allow the luxury of seeing their progress.

Kevin Warner's records from Lakeside crossed her desk, and she was pleased to learn that the young man's arm was healing well, thanks to his surgeon's painstaking efforts. With therapy, he'd eventually be removed from the disabled list.

On Friday morning Dana Mitchell had been her first patient.

'The burned areas are healing nicely,' Naomi told her after she'd examined her hands.

'I'm following your instructions to the letter,' Dana said. 'Thank goodness for the people who've helped me. I don't know what I would have done without them.'

'I'll arrange for some physical therapy. Another week and you should be able to resume your activities.'

'I always thought I'd enjoy having nothing to do,' Dana said, 'but I'm about to go crazy.'

'I know you're feeling better, but hang on a little longer,' Naomi advised. 'We don't want to create problems at this point.'

Dana agreed and Naomi left the room. Before she grabbed the next chart she overheard Joan, the receptionist, speaking on the telephone. 'He'll be happy to hear of your concern.'

She hung up the phone and grimaced. 'I bet the phone system is overloaded from all of the people wanting news about Dr Taylor.'

'If word of his aneurysm leaks out, it will be worse,' Naomi said. Following his collapse at the picnic, people were enquiring for the most recent update nearly every hour. Out of frustration and to ensure Hank's rest, Eloise had purchased an answering machine to deal with the distraction at home. The office staff, unfortunately, had to give each caller their personal attention.

'I'm praying it won't,' Joan said fervently.

Naomi hoped so, too, but she had her doubts. There were no secrets in a town this size—a novel concept after living in a big city where most people minded their own business.

'Who's next?' she asked.

'Dr Parker's seeing the last one.' The woman picked a scrap of paper off the desk. 'Gibbs' Pharmacy called about a prescription you wrote for Ruth Becker. Something about not having what you ordered in stock and could you make a substitution.'

'I'll call.' Naomi headed down the hallway to use the telephone in the small room that functioned both as supply closet and basic laboratory. After a discussion with the pharmacist she neared one of the patient cubicles and overheard a child's shrill cry.

She smiled, wondering how Adam dealt with recalcitrant children.

'No, Mommy,' a little girl shrieked. 'I don't want Dr Parker.'

A masculine voice answered, but Naomi couldn't

make out the words. 'Nao-o,' came the answer. 'Don't want him. Want the lady with the magic fingers.'

She froze in her tracks. The little voice sounded familiar.

Lettie came out of a room, her arms laden with pamphlets on prenatal care. 'What in the world is that child crying about?'

Naomi managed a weak grin but didn't answer. Instead, she opened the door a few inches. Although she hated to intrude on Adam and his patient, she was certain that she could calm the child, provided he hadn't already done so. She peeked inside to find Tina Newsome sitting on a woman's lap, hugging her casted arm to her chest in a protective manner. Tears streaked a trail down her flushed face.

'I told you about her, Mommy. The lady in the 'mergency place.'

'But she's not here, darling,' Mrs Newsome said. 'She told us to see Dr Parker.'

Naomi caught Adam's attention and he bolted off the counter. As he walked toward her she stepped into the corridor, giving him an apologetic smile.

His lab-jacketed shoulders seemed to fill the doorway and she was instantly transported to the time when she'd traced the lines and sinews of his back. Willing the thought away, she said, 'What's wrong with Tina?'

'I'm not sure because she won't let me touch her. Normally she doesn't make a fuss but today she keeps talking about someone with magic from ER. I'm trying to figure out who she's talking about but I'm drawing a blank.'

'I'm the one she wants.'

'No kidding?' His eyes widened.

She nodded. 'She wasn't co-operative when she came to ER with her broken arm so I showed her a coin trick. After that she was great.'

He stepped aside and extended his arm with a flourish. 'OK, Doctor. Let's see those magic fingers at work.'

Naomi walked in, digging in the pocket of her white coat for the coin. 'Hi, Tina.'

Tina squealed and bounced on her mother's lap. 'The magic doctor's here. Want to see the money disappear again.'

'After Dr Parker finds out what's wrong,' Naomi said firmly.

'Go ahead,' he told her, apparently unconcerned about placing his patient in her care. He leaned against the counter and struck a relaxed pose.

Naomi faced her patient. 'What's wrong with Tina today?'

'She's been fussing with the cast,' Mrs Newsome reported. 'She says it itches here.' She pointed to an area on the back of Tina's hand near her wrist.

Conscious of Adam monitoring her movements, Naomi examined her previous handiwork. The child's fingers were warm and pink as they should have been. 'Can you wiggle your fingers?'

Tina moved them with ease. No problem there.

Naomi straightened, puzzled. 'Did she have a bug bite before she broke her arm?'

'It's possible,' Mrs Newsome said. 'She plays outside a lot.'

Naomi glanced at Adam. He shrugged, clearly as stymied as she was. 'Maybe an X-ray will show us something. I'll call Radiology and tell them you're coming. After that, come back,' she instructed, wondering if it would be necessary to cut a window in the cast.

'Now can I see the magic?' Tina asked.

'Yes, you may.' Naomi withdrew the coin and, with a sleight of hand, made it disappear. Sensing Adam's interest, she walked over to him. 'I think Dr Parker has the coin.'

'Really?' Tina asked, her eyes wide.

'In fact, I'm sure of it.' Naomi reached toward his breast pocket and withdrew the shiny fifty-cent piece.

Tina clapped. In the next instant her cheerfulness faded. 'My magic doesn't work.'

'What do you mean?' Naomi asked.

'I can't get money to come out of my ears or my pockets or my arm.'

Naomi glanced at Adam. He straightened and his eyes lit up as if he shared her thoughts. 'Did you put any coins in your cast, Tina?' he asked.

She nodded. 'They disappeared like they're s'posed to, but they wouldn't come out. I tried and tried.'

Naomi took Tina's arm. 'Where did you put the money?'

Tina demonstrated. Naomi moved the girl's fingers to peer into the cast. Sure enough, she saw something silver.

'Tweezers,' she ordered. Adam held out a pair and she grabbed the handles. 'Thanks.' Careful not to poke Tina's skin, Naomi gripped the metal and tugged. 'Don't move, Tina.'

A few seconds later she withdrew a quarter, then another. 'How many pieces did you push into your cast?'

'Dunno.'

Naomi used a flashlight to help the search, but couldn't see anything. 'If there are more than the two pieces she shoved them up high enough that I can't find them.' She glanced at Adam. 'We'd better have an X-ray.'

He nodded.

Naomi turned to Mrs Newsome. 'I'll explain the situation to the radiology staff. If there aren't any more foreign objects you can go home. Otherwise, you'll need to bring her back. Along with the films.'

She crouched down to Tina's eye level. 'Remember, Tina, don't poke anything in your cast, again. OK?'

Tina's head bounced up and down. 'Won't.'

Mother and daughter left. Naomi sank weakly onto the exam table. 'I never dreamed she'd do something like that. I've shown hundreds of kids my trick and nothing like this has ever happened.'

At least not to her knowledge, she amended. There might easily have been several cases, but if the parents had taken the children to their family physicians the news wouldn't have filtered back to her.

'It was bound to some time,' Adam said. He grinned. 'At least I know who the doctor with the magic fingers is. When the youngsters hear about this I predict a rash of ailments. Be prepared to give a magic show.'

'I hope not,' she said fervently.

He winked. 'Of course, I wouldn't mind a private demonstration.'

Certain that his thoughts were as racy as hers, her face warmed. 'Maybe. Someday.'

'I'll look forward to it. So, how do you like family practice?'

The change in subject caught her off guard. 'Fine. It

has its moments.' She grinned. 'Like with Tina.'

His smile was slow and lazy and reminded her of the expression on his face before he'd kissed her. 'Do you know something?'

'What?'

'You're wasted in ER.'

CHAPTER SEVEN

'I BEG your pardon?' Naomi asked.

Adam looked thoughtful. 'I'm surprised you didn't go into Pediatrics.'

'Sorry to disappoint you,' she said lightly.

'Why didn't you?'

She shrugged. 'I preferred the variety of emergency medicine, the new faces constantly coming through.'

'I guess that's why I didn't care for it,' he said. 'I want to know my patients and them to know me.'

'Trauma work isn't for everyone,' she agreed.

'Do you ever get tired of it? The stabbings, the gunshot wounds, the car accidents? Never knowing how your patients are doing once they leave?'

She thought for a moment. She'd sutured gashes, prescribed antibiotics and performed any one of a hundred medical procedures on more people than she could possibly remember, but she rarely saw them again. If a patient did weigh on her mind she banished the thought as quickly as possible.

That was the way she wanted it—she'd convinced herself of that years ago.

'Occasionally I do,' she admitted. 'But, then, I'm sure you get tired of certain aspects of your practice, too.'

'Not often, but there are times. . .' He sat in the spare chair and stretched out his legs in a picture of relaxation. 'Tell me about Naomi Stewart.'

She tensed. 'What do you want to know?'

'Your childhood. Your dreams. Whatever you want to tell.'

She drew a deep breath. 'My growing-up years were tough. My dad had a few problems—' she edited out his involvement with alcohol '—so he didn't work much. My brother and I helped Mom with what we could. We delivered newspapers, mowed lawns, baby-sat, shoveled snow. You name it, we did it. Mark was good at ferreting out odd jobs for us.'

'I'll bet you were a natural leader in school.'

She smiled. 'I was painfully shy, although there were four of us who became close friends. We had a lot in common so we stuck together.

'I had these horrible horn-rimmed glasses that I hated but there wasn't enough money for a new pair. I needed braces, too. I started saving money in high school and then, when I turned eighteen, I worked two minimum-wage jobs. My earnings paid for contact lenses and to fix my overbite. Luckily, learning came easy and scholarships paid for most of my education.'

'No wonder you're so independent.'

'Don't make it sound like a curse,' she said.

'I'm not. Just making an observation.' He looked thoughtful. 'Hank tells me you won't be coming to the barbecue we're having tomorrow night.'

Once again he'd changed the conversation in mid-stream. She was beginning to feel as though she were undergoing an interview. 'I thought I'd stay home. Relax. Enjoy the peace and quiet. Do my nails.' She made a mental note to stop at the family-owned drug store and buy a bottle of polish. The last time she'd painted her fingernails had been for Kirsten's and Jake's wedding last Christmas.

'Besides,' she continued, 'it sounded like a family get-together.' With Hank facing major surgery, the close-knit Parker family would want to spend time doting on the man who'd played such a significant role in their lives. She didn't want to intrude on his moment.

'He thinks of you as a daughter, you know.'

She froze. 'He does?'

'Carrie died as a child. He says you remind him of what he'd thought she'd be if she'd grown up.'

One of the so-called workaholics? She doubted it. Instead, she fell silent as she studied the floor tiles. What *could* she say?

'He needs his friends around him. It's probably hard for you to understand that, not being used to having close friends or family nearby.'

His accurate assessment surprised her and she stared at him, speechless.

'The real riches in life are our families and the relationships we have with them.'

She stiffened. 'I'm afraid I disagree.'

'Then you believe money can buy happiness?'

'No, but—' She stopped short. Did he think that she worked hard for her promotion because she was only interested in the financial freedom it would give her? That she'd have more buying power to amass *things*?

He did, she realized, remembering his look of disdain at her dress and the way he'd frozen when he'd seen her car. He'd obviously put her in the same self-centered class as Cynthia, and the idea stung.

'What I meant to say was that your belief is probably true in a functional family unit. There are many that aren't.'

Her own was a fine example. She'd never known her

grandparents, her father had disappeared when she was twelve, her mother had died and her brother had joined the service. Work was all she had, not counting Kirsten and Beth.

A thought came to her—one that nearly took her breath away. Were her limited personal relationships a result of her single-minded determination to succeed, or was she hiding behind her career to avoid those same relationships?

She'd have to think about it.

Several minutes elapsed. His intent gaze held an understanding she hadn't seen before in him, and she felt as if he read her innermost thoughts.

'Sorry to interrupt,' Mary said from the doorway, 'but I thought you'd like to hear Tina's Radiology report. No foreign objects.'

'Thanks, Mary,' Naomi said, grateful for the opportunity to focus on someone other than herself. Adam, however, refused to let the subject drop.

'Don't shut him out, Naomi,' he said softly. 'Not now.'

Swinging her braid over her shoulder, she swallowed hard. Much as she hated to admit it, she and Hank had a lot in common. Perhaps that's why he'd wriggled his way into her heart so quickly.

'OK,' she whispered. It would be hard to undo old habits but she'd do her best.

'Then you'll come?'

She gave him a resigned smile. 'Yes.'

Adam drove to the hospital for his evening rounds with his mind on his newest partner. Ever since the picnic he'd begun to question the opinions he'd held concerning her. This afternoon, however, he'd revised it completely, finally understanding her motives.

No wonder she was driven to succeed—she'd obviously dreamed of overcoming her underprivileged background and had worked hard to achieve her goal. The supervisor position at Lakeside was simply one more step in her effort to put those years behind her. The expensive purchases she'd made no longer bothered him—her motives and Cynthia's were as far apart as east and west.

At the same time she'd never wipe away the lessons she'd learned, no matter how many new cars or fancy dresses she bought. She still had a sense of frugality— why else would she buy designer-copy fragrances rather than the expensive originals?

He grinned, remembering how she'd held Tina's attention with the coin trick. He and Hank had a good rapport with their young patients, but he couldn't recall having ever seen the total look of rapture on a child's face as he'd seen today.

He'd been entranced as well, although it hadn't been because of the trick. No, it was watching her slim fingers handle the piece of silver that had done it. At the time, he'd mentally replayed the incident of her hands on his back—kneading his muscles, caressing his skin as his mouth had covered hers.

The memory evoked the same physical response as if she'd repeated the unplanned and thoroughly delightful intimacy in the flesh. He wanted more than a memory— he wanted the actual experience of making love with this woman.

Tina had been right. Naomi *was* the doctor with the magic fingers.

He shifted position to ease his private ache and flexed his shoulders, willing his body to normal. Traveling at thirty miles an hour was not the time to indulge in fantasy or wishful thinking.

Rounding a corner, he knew that his original reservations about her acting as a locum had disappeared. Naomi had fitted in with the rest of the office staff almost immediately. The transition couldn't have gone any more smoothly if he'd planned it which, in spite of it being his habit, he hadn't.

Heat blasted him as he unfolded himself out of his air-conditioned Cherokee and hurried into the cool building. In his haste he took the stairs two at a time to reach the third floor.

As he rounded the corner of the first flight he ran into his aunt. 'Rachel! Finally calling it a day?'

'I've been meaning to talk to you,' Rachel said without replying to his pleasantry. 'We have a problem.'

'With what?'

'With Dr Stewart.'

'What's wrong?'

Rachel tapped her foot. 'With the records. She simply refuses to complete the charts correctly. I've asked her to follow our protocol but she doesn't listen to me.'

Adam narrowed his eyes. 'That doesn't sound like Naomi.'

'Hmm.' Rachel crossed her arms. 'Have you read any of her medical records?'

'No.'

'Then maybe it's time you did. I won't be responsible if there's a lawsuit.' She narrowed her eyes. 'Is it true she's taking Hank's place in your office?'

'Yes.'

'You're making a big mistake,' she warned. 'Dr Stewart doesn't belong here.'

Sensing that his aunt was about to launch into a familiar gloom-and-doom tirade, he tried to end the conversation. 'Your comments are duly noted. As for the chart-keeping, I'll talk to her.'

'See that you do. Goodnight, Adam.' Her heels clicked on the steps as she descended the stairs.

Adam went on his way, certain that Rachel was being difficult to please. Naomi didn't strike him as being lax about documentation, but he'd mention Rachel's record-keeping idiosyncrasies to avoid further conflicts.

Lacey stood by the gas grill as Adam checked the shish-kebabs of meat and vegetables lying on the hot grate. 'So, brother, dear, how has work been?'

Adam closed the lid and hung the long fork on the handle. 'Fine.'

Lacey tipped her head toward the patio where Naomi, Lettie, Dale and Hank were engaged in conversation. 'Lettie seems quite taken with Naomi.'

He grinned. 'I never thought I'd see the day when anyone made a positive, instantaneous impression on Lettie.'

'What happened?'

'Right after I introduced the two of them Naomi told her how much she was looking forward to relying on Lettie's experience since she didn't know the people like Lettie and Hank did. Once she mentioned that she was depending on her Lettie was putty in her hands.' He shook his head, remembering. 'I've never seen anything like it.'

Lettie had nodded, appeared pleased and had instantly became Naomi's ally.

'Certainly not the same reaction as when she met Cynthia,' Lacey commented.

'Not a bit.' Cynthia had brushed Lettie off as a nurse with antiquated skills and had treated her as such. Although few dared to voice their opinion or show their delight once she'd moved on to more lucrative pastures, the atmosphere in the office had lightened considerably. After he'd recovered from his feelings of rejection he'd realized his good fortune.

'Yes,' he continued, 'Naomi is a nice addition to our group.'

'What a shame.'

Lacey's mournful expression caught him by surprise. 'I thought you'd be thrilled.'

'I'm not.' She grinned. 'I miss having her around so I was hoping you'd send her back to ER.'

'Forget it,' he declared. 'She's mine.'

The question in Lacey's eyes and the smirk on her face made him realize how possessive he'd sounded. 'Until Hank gets on his feet again.'

Unbidden, his gaze went to his mentor. Hank was smiling but Adam saw how fragile and frail he looked.

'He'll be as good as new,' Lacey began.

Adam interrupted, unwilling to contemplate the alternative. 'Of course he will. I'll make sure of it, even if I have to camp beside his bed the entire time.'

'How long a recovery period do you think he'll need?'

He shrugged. 'It depends. Abdominal surgery is major so at least a month. Even then, he won't be able to resume his normal load for a while.'

'And if he never does?'

Adam didn't answer. He lifted the lid to check the food, ignoring the irritation in his eyes caused by the rolling cloud of smoke. Once he'd turned the kebabs he closed the lid again. 'Then we'll find a permanent partner.'

He'd always thought of that event in terms of the distant future, and had planned to offer Hank's share to one of the locums who'd helped in the past. Unfortunately, the distant future was closer to the present than he'd like, and the locums he knew no longer seemed like partner material.

'What about Naomi?' she asked.

'She'd be great. Wonderful, in fact. Convincing her to stay, though, would require an act of Congress. She has her heart set on the promotion at Lakeside.'

'It would be an honor,' she said, 'but you don't want her selected, do you?'

He rubbed his eyes. 'No.' He had nothing against her professional advancement; he simply had compelling reasons for wanting her to stay in Deer Creek. Personal reasons that had nothing to do with her skills as a physician and everything to do with her being a woman.

'As I said before, you'll have to give her an incentive to remain.'

'Becoming a shift supervisor has been a goal of hers for a long time. She won't give it up easily,' he warned.

Lacey shrugged. 'Who said anything about easy?' She furrowed her brow in thought. 'You won't fix the situation to suit yourself, will you?'

'Wait a minute—' he interrupted.

'You often do,' she insisted. 'But you can't this time.

It has to be her decision, and if you take it out of her hands you'll lose her for sure.'

Staring across the yard at Naomi, surrounded by his family, he slowly nodded. 'I know.'

'She isn't another sister you can boss around. We know you mean well so we've learned to bear it.' She punched him lightly on the arm. 'But you can't treat her like you treat us.'

'I know.' As he thought about Lacey's statement his smile suddenly grew broader and he winked. 'I don't want to either.'

Naomi leaned back in the cushioned chair and drew in a deep breath. Adam couldn't have chosen a finer evening for his barbecue. The temperature hovered in the nineties and the shade created by the patio cover provided welcome relief. A slight breeze occasionally stirred the air and birds chirped their songs as the sun's rays began to weaken.

The company was as enjoyable as the weather. She'd tried to hang on the fringe of the gathering but Mrs Parker hadn't allowed it. She had found herself at Hank's right hand most of the time.

At nine o'clock Hank pleaded exhaustion and, as Eloise had chauffeured both him and Naomi, Eloise drove him home. Naomi tried to leave at the same time but Hank insisted that she stayed. Before she could argue everything had been decided. Gradually the other guests left until only Adam, Melissa, Lacey and Dale, Rosie and Naomi remained.

'Get enough to eat?' Adam asked, selecting a place next to her in the circle formed by their chairs.

'You bet. The food was delicious. I won't need to eat for a week.'

'So, Adam,' Melissa said, 'when are you ever going to replace that horrid wallpaper in your dining room?'

'It's not too bad. Sort of grows on you,' he said.

'Like a fungus,' Melissa agreed. 'I always thought you had better taste than that.'

'What's wrong with leafy vines?' he asked.

Lacey rolled her eyes. 'Nothing if you're Tarzan of the Jungle.'

'I suppose you'd choose some wild geometric print,' he said.

Melissa shook her head. 'No. You need stripes and solids in a deep color. Burgundy and hunter green.'

'I presume you have something picked out?' he asked wryly.

Melissa nodded. 'I saw it when I was in Kansas City the other day car-shopping. The design fits you to a T; it would look great in your house.'

'Are you willing to hang it for me?' he asked.

'I might be persuaded,' Melissa answered.

Naomi listened to their interchange with interest. It reminded her of the discussions she'd had with her close friends, Beth, Kirsten and Ellen. She missed those days—the times spent with the girls who'd been like sisters to her.

To a certain extent they still were, although Ellen had since died and both Beth and Kirsten were married and working on families of their own. They continued to call each other or write letters on a regular basis but long-distance friendships were hard to maintain. A sudden wave of homesickness came over her—not for her home but for her friends.

'Is something wrong?' Adam asked.

She pulled her thoughts together. 'No. Why do you ask?'

'You looked like you were a million miles away.'

'Not that many. Just a few hundred,' she said.

Adam spoke to Melissa. 'What did you say about car-shopping?'

'I've been looking,' she admitted.

'For what?'

'A sports car. Preferably an import.'

'Who sells imports in Deer Creek?' Mrs Parker asked.

'No one. I've been looking out of town. In fact, I've picked out this little red car that's an absolute dream,' Melissa said proudly.

'And who will service it when it needs repair?' Adam asked.

'The dealer.'

'And what if your dream car's undrivable? How do you intend to get it there? Tow it?'

'If I have to.' Melissa's jaw took on a stubborn tilt.

'Do you realize how expensive—?'

'Yes, Adam,' Melissa said, 'I've considered the cost.'

Lacey joined in. 'You have a foreign car.'

'Yes, but Jake at the Speedy Service station can manage most of the repairs.'

Melissa turned to her mother. 'What do you think?'

Mrs Parker's eyes twinkled. 'Adam's brought up some good points. I'm sure you'll consider them carefully.'

'I have. If I stick to the recommended maintenance schedule I shouldn't have any problems,' Melissa said.

Adam pursed his lips, as if considering. 'I suppose it's

possible,' he said slowly, 'but the risks are still high.'

Melissa leaned forward. 'I really want to do this, Adam. Risks or no risks. I'll have to live with my decision. Not you.'

'You heard her, folks,' he said to those assembled. 'If her little red pride and joy develops a mechanical glitch she won't call any of us.'

Naomi smiled as everyone laughed.

'That's not what I meant,' Melissa protested.

'OK, OK.' Adam's humor gave way to seriousness. 'Will you at least let me come with you? Make sure you get a good price and a car that isn't a factory reject?'

Melissa smiled. 'It's a date. When can we go?'

'How about next week? We'll be in Kansas City anyway.'

'Perfect. I'll drive Hank home from the hospital.' Melissa's eyes sparkled with excitement and she wriggled in her lawn chair. 'He'll love it—it's the color of candy apples and can go from zero to fifty in nothing flat.' She snapped her fingers.

'I'm sure the highway patrol will be impressed,' Adam said wryly.

'I'll watch my speed,' she said. 'I always do.'

'Always?' Adam asked in disbelief. 'I seem to recall a ticket not too long ago. . .'

Melissa leaned over to Naomi. 'I get one ticket in twenty-seven years and he won't let me forget.'

'Of course not. I loaned you the money to pay it.'

Naomi smiled and hid a yawn behind her hand as Mrs Parker rose. 'Time for me to go. It's getting late.'

The party broke up and everyone headed for their vehicles. With Lacey's house a few blocks away from

Hank's, Naomi was ready to beg a ride but before she could make her request Adam spoke up.

'I'll drive you home,' he announced, sending an unspoken signal to Dale. Before she knew it she found herself alone with Adam.

'You have a lovely home,' she said to cover up her sudden shyness.

'Have the girls given you a tour?'

'No,' she said, anxious to explore every nook and cranny of the two-story, early twentieth-century home for herself.

'Then let's go.' He led the way inside, through the patio doors and into the kitchen. 'I modernized this room first because I couldn't stand the lack of electrical outlets and antiquated plumbing.'

She admired the oak cabinets lining one wall, the modern appliances and the counter-top island in the center of the work space.

Gradually he worked his way through the first floor, showing off the living room, a parlor and his office. 'The woodwork has all been restored to its original condition. My sisters and I did most of it,' he said proudly.

'It's beautiful.'

He led her toward the staircase and she oohed over the curving oak banister, polished to a high sheen. 'I can see a rambunctious little boy sliding down this,' she said, lightly touching the well-worn wood with her fingertips as she ascended the stairs.

'Not a rambunctious little girl?'

She laughed. 'Her, too.'

Her last step brought her to a cozy nook with a large eastern window. Swedish ivy and a Boston fern hung from wall hooks, strategically placed to capture the morning sunlight. It was a perfect reading corner on dreary days.

'There are four bedrooms,' he said. 'One is mine, another is for guests and two are used for storage. Someday, when I need the extra living space, I'll clean those two out.'

'What made you choose such a big house?'

'It was the only thing available when I was looking to buy a place of my own. Also, the price was right.'

'Well, it's wonderful.'

From the hallway she saw the masculine shades of burgundy and blue decorating his room and walked inside. The king-sized four-poster bed dominating the room immediately caught her eye and she gasped. She imagined his trousers hitched over one post, his bare torso lying among the twisted navy sheets, one well-muscled leg bent and uncovered. The mattress would be firm like its owner and she felt an odd urge to sit on the bed and test it for herself.

Naomi swallowed, inching away before she gave in to her impulse. She stole a glance at Adam and realized that she'd shortened the distance between them. The lazy look in his eyes as he captured her gaze suggested that his imagination was as fertile as hers.

The digital clock beside his bed changed to twelve o'clock. If she stayed in this charged atmosphere a moment longer she knew where they'd spend the rest of the evening.

'Look at the time. Hank will be wondering where I'm at.'

'Don't you think he'll know?' His grin was lopsided.

'Yes, but I don't want him to think—'

'Stay.'

'I can't.' She begged him with her eyes to understand.

'Why not?'

'I don't do one-nighters.'

'Neither do I.'

Naomi stared at him. 'What are you saying?'

'I believe in a commitment. I'm old-fashioned in that respect.'

'And if I can't give you one?'

'Then dance with me.'

'No music,' she pointed out.

Adam opened a cabinet in one corner of the room to reveal a stereo system. He selected a compact disk and—with a push of a button—soft, sultry sounds filled the air.

'Who said there wasn't any music?' He walked toward her, slowly and deliberately, until he stood within arm's reach. 'Shall we?'

She moved into his embrace and he brought her to his chest. Immediately her reservations vanished and she melted against him. The music flowed over and around them as they swayed in time to its gentle beat.

His masculine scent hung in the air like a sweet, sensual aroma. 'You smell good,' she murmured.

'You do, too.' He held her hand tighter and placed it against his heart.

She felt the steady thump. Her analytical mind noticed that the rate was fast and his breaths short, and the feminine side of her took great pleasure in her observations.

He nipped at her ear lobe and a strange tremor shot through her. She heard a moan and an answering groan of male satisfaction. Her skin burned under his touch.

Oh, my, she thought in what seemed like slow motion. He hadn't even kissed her yet and already she was falling apart at the seams.

The song ended and he stepped back abruptly. For a few seconds she stared at him and he at her until he ran his hand over his hair. His grin was slow. 'You're pretty potent, Dr Stewart.'

She willed her breathing back to normal. 'So are you, Dr Parker.'

'I'd better take you home, unless. . .' He raised one eyebrow.

She glanced at the bed and its beckoning depths. Yet she couldn't sacrifice her principles for a few hours of physical bliss. 'It is late,' she said softly.

He walked beside her down the wide staircase. His hand lingered on the small of her back and was enough to keep her senses heightened and aware of the embers smoldering between them.

Within minutes he'd buckled her into his Cherokee and backed out of the driveway. 'Aren't you glad you came?'

'Yes, I am,' she said, realizing that she meant it. 'Although I'm amazed how you manage to keep tabs on your sisters the way you do.'

'It keeps me busy,' he admitted. 'But part of it's habit, part of it is because they expect me to and part of it is that I don't want us to drift apart. After they're married we will—to a certain degree, anyway—but I'm holding off the inevitable. Hopefully, by then I'll have a wife who'll be my priority.'

The idea of Adam married disturbed her. 'Do you have someone in mind?' she asked lightly, trying to keep her feelings from showing.

He shrugged. 'A person never knows when Mr or Ms Right will show up.'

'True.'

Adam turned onto Birchwood Lane and drove a few blocks toward Hank's home. As the car lights illuminated the paved road Naomi noticed a pile of fur lying in the middle. She straightened and pointed at it.

'What's that?' she asked, instinctively knowing what it was.

'Looks like an animal of some sort. A cat maybe.'

'No, I don't think so.' Naomi craned her head to study the animal as Adam drove past. The body lay in a contorted heap, its characteristic bushy tail now limp.

A lump came to her throat and she settled back against the seat cushion. She stared straight ahead, saddened by the sight and angered over her emotional turmoil. She had no business crying over a wild animal, even though this one had a special place in her heart.

It was Lester.

CHAPTER EIGHT

'LOOKS like a squirrel,' Adam remarked.

'Yeah.' Naomi swallowed hard. She dug her fingernails into her palm, hoping that Adam would change the subject.

'He must have dashed across the street,' he continued. 'They're quick but sometimes they don't make it. I wonder if it's one of those that play in Hank's yard.'

'I'm sure it is.' Her voice squeaked and she cleared her throat.

He parked the car in the drive. Impatient to leave before she embarrassed herself with tears and had to explain, she tugged on the handle. 'Thanks for the ride,' she said, but the doors were electronically locked and wouldn't budge.

He leaned back in the seat to study her. 'You're upset over the squirrel, aren't you?'

She stared through the windshield, wishing that the light on Hank's garage had burned out. 'Why should I be?'

He waited and she felt compelled to divert his attention as best she could.

'It's only a dumb animal. He should have known better than to run in front of a moving vehicle. Lester was just too daring for his own good. He should have been more like Lizzie.'

Lizzie had always eyed them warily, scampering away if they got too close. Lester, on the other hand, was more trusting. Although he kept out of actual reach he would often come within a few feet of them.

'Maybe he didn't believe someone would hurt him,' Adam said softly.

'Then he wasn't very smart,' she declared. 'People— things,' she corrected, 'get hurt all the time in one way or another. Now Lizzie has to carry on without him.' After a brief hesitation she glanced directly at him. 'Do you suppose they mourn their companions' passing?'

He shrugged. 'I wouldn't know. The subject never came up in my biology classes, and if it did I missed it.' He paused for a fraction of a second. 'We're talking about something else besides squirrels, aren't we?'

She sighed. 'Forget I said anything. These things happen. No big deal.' She scolded herself for giving human traits and emotions to a wild animal who functioned by instinct and not reason.

'Losing anyone isn't easy,' he agreed. 'But you go on. You have to.'

She shifted position to lean against the door rather than the seat. 'Hank's been on my mind a lot lately.'

His voice seemed far away. 'Mine, too.'

'Have you discussed what you'll do if he doesn't bounce back from this surgery?'

Adam rested his arms on top of the steering-wheel. 'Only in general terms. We're being optimistic.'

'As you should be, but it doesn't hurt to have a plan to fall back on—even a sketchy one.'

'We do, but it involves you.'

'Me?'

He hesitated. 'I want you to consider something during the next few weeks.'

A sense of foreboding fell upon her. 'What's that?'

'Staying in Deer Creek on a permanent basis.'

She'd been afraid he'd ask that very question. 'You don't need an ER supervisor.'

'No, but the community can always use a good doctor.'

'You're looking for someone else. You said so on several occasions,' she reminded him.

'I did, but no one seemed to be what I was looking for.'

'And you think I am?' she asked, incredulous.

He met her gaze. 'After what happened at my house you can ask that?'

She shook her head, hardly believing what he'd said.

'We'd make a good partnership.'

'What sort of partners? Business?'

'For starters. I think it could easily develop into something more personal, don't you think?' He covered her hand with his.

'Yes, but. . .' Her voice died. The idea was exciting and frightening as she'd lived most of her life shunning close relationships.

'I've always thought of myself in terms of my career,' she said slowly. 'I've never made time for or considered anything else.'

'Maybe you should. I know the decision to leave Lakeside would be tough to make but all I'm asking is for you to think about it.'

She hated being put on the spot but, to be truthful, she did enjoy her work in Deer Creek. It was different from the hustle and bustle in Kansas City, and the slower pace was nice for a change. The chemistry between herself and Adam made for an added bonus, but was it enough?

She loved her assignment at Lakeside's Emergency Services. How could she possibly choose between the two? How could she give up a sure career when a relationship with Adam was so uncertain? At a loss for words, she toyed with the fringe of her braid and studied his dashboard.

'No pressure. Just open yourself to the possibility. Will you at least promise me that much?'

She dropped her hands into her lap and glanced at him. 'Yes.'

His grin of satisfaction made her wary. 'Don't raise your hopes too high,' she warned. 'I'll probably disappoint you.'

'I'm hoping neither of us will be disappointed.' With that, he unfolded his long legs out of the vehicle, came around and opened her door, then escorted her to the front entrance.

'Thanks again for a nice evening,' she said.

'Sleep well,' he said before he bent his head and brushed his mouth against hers. In the next instant he was gone.

Adam's step was light as he went through the side door of Hank's garage. Naomi would never know how tense he'd been—how he'd debated the best way to ask her to consider remaining in Deer Creek. But after this evening he was glad that everything had fallen into place. He'd suspected that there would be sparks between them but he'd never dreamed that those sparks would burst into a conflagration so quickly.

The next few weeks would be crucial to her decision and he aimed to show her what a fine team, both professionally and personally, they would make.

He flicked on the light switch and strode toward the corner where Hank kept a shovel. With the implement in hand, he found a small box with a lid, before retracing his steps to the door.

Hank had always told him never to give up his dream and that advice had kept him going on many occasions, especially when he'd wanted to forget the idea of medical school. Naomi followed her dream with the same tenacity, and now it was Adam's job not to take away her dream but to give her a better one.

As he strode down the sidewalk, illuminated by the streetlamps, he hoped that he'd be successful.

In spite of Adam's suggestion, Naomi didn't sleep well. The subject of a career in Deer Creek versus one in Lakeside preyed on her mind until she couldn't think straight any more. As soon as the sun's rays broke through the curtains of her east-facing window she rose and crept from the house. A brisk walk on a quiet Sunday morning would clear the cobwebs from her brain.

Without thinking, she started out in her usual direction until she realized that she'd see Lester. She almost turned around, then decided against it. After seeing trauma cases in ER, she could handle seeing a dead squirrel.

She came to the area but the carcass was gone. Puzzled, she scanned the street, thinking that she'd misidentified the area. Finally, she noticed a dark smudge on the pavement—this was definitely the spot.

Wondering who had removed Lester's remains, the answer came before she'd finished the question. Adam had done it. He'd known how the animal's demise had affected her and he'd tried to shield her from the pain.

His thoughtfulness touched her. She couldn't remember anyone in recent memory being so concerned about her mental well-being. She'd had an inkling before but now she knew.

She loved him.

As the days went by Naomi found it difficult enough to keep up with the present, much less consider her future.

The morning of Hank's surgery dawned and she awoke feeling edgy and impatient. Then again, she shouldn't have been surprised. She'd star-gazed into the early hours of the morning because she'd had trouble sleeping, and even after she'd gone to bed she'd only dozed.

The telephone rang halfway through her breakfast of corn flakes and milk. Realistically, it was too early for word about Hank but she couldn't stop the sudden trepidation from rolling over her.

'I have an older woman in ER,' Lacey began without preamble. 'You need to see her right away. She's complaining of rectal bleeding. I checked and her occult blood is positive.'

As the test result was abnormal a gastrointestinal disorder popped into Naomi's mind first. Bleeding into the GI tract was serious and demanded immediate medical attention. 'Order a CBC, along with a type and crossmatch for four units. I'm on my way.'

The full moon must have affected a lot of residents, she decided as she rinsed the cereal bowl and tipped it on the drainboard. The monthly cycle always seemed to make the natives restless, and she predicted busy days ahead. Vaguely she wondered if any of Adam's maternity patients were due.

She grabbed a blueberry muffin, along with her purse, on her way out the door and walked into ER ten minutes later.

'How long has this been going on?' Naomi asked Edith Stone, a fifty-year-old, slightly overweight brunette with threads of silver running through her hair.

'It started yesterday,' Edith said.

'Are you having any other symptoms?'

She shook her head.

'What medications are you taking?'

'None.' Edith avoided Naomi's eyes, a fact which didn't go unnoticed.

Naomi performed her examination, noticing several blue and purple marks on Edith's arms and legs. 'Have you had any episodes like this before?'

Edith shook her head again.

'How did you get the bruises, Edith?' she asked, trying to make sense of the symptoms and wondering if this was a case of domestic violence. She glanced at Lacey with a question in her eyes and Lacey answered her with a shrug.

'I didn't do anything.' Edith was a picture of dejection; her shoulders were slumped and her face was drawn.

Naomi sat on the bed next to Edith. 'How are things at home?'

Her question opened a floodgate of emotions. Edith burst into tears and buried her face in her hands.

'We've been married for thirty years,' she sobbed, 'and that, that *worm* I married asked for a divorce two days ago. On our anniversary, no less.'

Naomi patted her shoulder.

'I was so depressed.' Lacey handed Edith a tissue. The woman hiccuped and blew her nose. 'Anyway, I did a really dumb thing.'

'Which was?' Naomi coaxed.

'We had some rat poison in the garage.' Edith's voice died away.

Naomi knew what would come next. 'Did you eat some?'

Edith's chin quivered. She nodded. 'Several hours later I realized that I couldn't give up so easily. After all I've done for that man I refuse to die and let him have everything I've worked for without a fight.'

She drew a tremulous breath. 'I made myself vomit and thought everything would be fine. That was the night before last, but then this. . .' she held out her arms to reveal her light purple blotches '. . .happened and I was so scared. I didn't know what to do so I came here.'

Naomi rose. 'You did the right thing. Now that I know what's wrong we can start the proper treatment.' She turned to Lacey. 'I want a urinalysis, stat. Call the lab and see if they have enough blood to perform coagulation studies, especially a prothrombin time. If not, draw another sample. We'll also transfuse several units of fresh frozen plasma as soon as possible.'

Lacey nodded and moved to the phone to place the call.

'You see, Edith,' Naomi told her, 'the rat poison prevents your blood from clotting and so you bleed profusely, which is how it kills the rodents. It's similar to the warfarin medication we routinely use as a blood thinner.'

'Is there something you can do?'

'We'll do everything we can to reverse the process but we need to determine how badly you've been affected.'

Edith nodded.

Lacey interrupted. 'The lab has enough blood. We should have a report in about twenty minutes.'

Naomi calculated the time-frame involved. 'The result we get now should be the peak value. Do you recall the name of the product you used?'

'No. It said something about super-strength.'

Naomi revised her thinking. If Edith had indeed swallowed a compound from the 'super-warfarin' group she could have problems for several weeks.

'In the meantime, Edith, I'm going to admit you.'

'You can't!' Edith was aghast. 'Everyone will know.'

'You don't have a choice. You'll require close monitoring.' At the mulish set to Edith's face, Naomi tried to appease her. 'You can request to withhold your name from the daily hospital press release.'

'OK,' she agreed. 'And I don't want that conniving man I married near me.'

'I'll tell the nurses to put a "no visitors" sign on your door and keep a close watch,' Naomi promised.

Before long Naomi had the lab reports in her hand and was explaining Edith's condition to her. 'Your hemoglobin is significantly low and there are red cells in your urine. Your coagulation results are over two hundred seconds which isn't good, considering it normally should be eleven or twelve seconds.

'I'm going to administer a vitamin K injection. The poison interferes with the liver's production of vitamin-K-dependent coagulation factors so you need extra amounts of the vitamin to compensate. You'll also receive a transfusion of fresh frozen plasma, which is a blood product rich in the clotting factor proteins.'

'When can I leave?'

'After I see a marked improvement and the danger of complications has passed.' Naomi softened her voice. 'I'm also recommending that a counselor visit with you before you're released.' She wasn't about to send the woman home unsupervised so that she could try overdosing again in another depressed moment. Edith seemed rather firm in her resolve but depression was a funny thing and Naomi refused to take any chances.

A nurse from the medical ward arrived to take Edith to a private room and Naomi sent the case notes with them. 'I'll be by to check on you later today, Edith.'

Naomi hurried to the office. With Adam taking the day off to be with Hank, she had her work cut out for her.

Her next case was a woman in her early thirties. 'I'd like this mole removed,' Lynda Akers said, pointing to an area on the calf of her left leg. 'It's never bothered me but it isn't the same color any more. I've always heard that a person should be alert to changes so I wanted someone to check it.'

Naomi studied the raised spot which was about the size of a thumbtack. The edges were hard and, as Lynda had mentioned, varied in color from red to blue to black.

Warning bells clanged in Naomi's mind. 'I could remove it but I'd rather you saw a specialist—a dermatologist.'

'Do you think it's cancer?'

'It could be a melanoma,' Naomi admitted, 'but the diagnosis can't be made without a biopsy. I don't want to disturb the cells any more than necessary, which is why I want a dermatologist involved.'

Lynda's eyes grew wide. 'Oh, my gosh. This sounds more serious than I thought.'

'I'm only informing you of the possibilities. We won't know for certain until we get a lab report.'

'If it is, what are my chances?'

'It all depends on how deeply the cells have invaded the skin. You've obviously been watching it closely so if my suspicions *are* correct we've caught it early.'

Naomi moved to the door. 'Wait here while I make an appointment for you.' Within minutes she returned and handed a piece of paper to Lynda. 'You're scheduled to see Dr Shapiro the day after tomorrow. Here's the address in Kansas City.'

'I've heard of him. He's good, isn't he?'

'One of the best,' Naomi said, knowing the importance of a patient's confidence in his or her physician. 'You're lucky to get in so quickly. Sometimes people have to wait weeks.' She grinned. 'It pays to know people.'

As Lynda left Naomi was excited at the prospect of following this case. She'd know Lynda's diagnosis and treatment well before she had to choose between Deer Creek and Lakeside.

She fingered the coin in her pocket. At the time she'd agreed to consider joining Adam's practice she'd planned to weigh the matter carefully and logically before arriving at her decision. After all, her whole life had been built around advancing her career. She'd always pictured herself as someone reaching the top of her field.

But that had been before she'd fallen in love with Adam. Even though her feelings had blossomed overnight, she hadn't expanded her mental picture to include him and she knew why.

She was afraid. She'd been deserted by family, one by one, starting with her father. Her chances of it happening again had to be phenomenal and she didn't want to experience those feelings of rejection again.

Later, while holding a twelve-month-old baby—the same age as Beth's daughter—she saw how lonely her picture was.

As she patted the little girl's well-padded bottom, admired the frilly yellow sunsuit her doting mother had dressed her in and smelled the sweet scent of baby it wasn't difficult to expand her vision to include an infant of her own. In an old house resembling Adam's.

Still, she couldn't swallow the bitter taste of fear in her mouth.

Naomi handed the child back to her mother. 'She's doing fine. Lettie will give her the diphtheria, pertussis and tetanus immunization, along with the oral polio vaccine. After that you're free to go.'

Mary stopped her in the hallway. 'Dr Parker's on line two.'

Naomi glanced at her watch. 'With good news, I hope.'

'He wouldn't say, but we're dying to know.'

Naomi picked up the nearest phone. 'Hi, Adam.'

Adam's voice came across weary but triumphant. 'The surgery went well. They moved Hank into Intensive Care just a few minutes ago.'

She sagged against the wall, unaware until that moment how tightly strung she'd been while waiting for word. 'So there weren't any problems?'

'None but, according to the surgeon, the weakened

portion of artery was starting to seep. Another week might have been too late.'

'Then we have two reasons to celebrate.'

'Yeah. Anyway, Hank should make a full recovery.'

'I'm glad.'

'I'm going to stick around for a while longer. Mom and Eloise are staying but I'll be coming home. How are things going?'

'Hectic but smooth, if that makes any sense.'

He laughed. 'Yeah, it does. See you in a few hours.'

Naomi replaced the receiver, feeling light-hearted. She rounded the corner of the hallway, to find Mary and Lettie lying in wait.

'Well?' Lettie demanded.

Her smile was broad. 'Hank's doing fine and should be back on his feet in no time.'

Lettie closed her eyes and raised her face to heaven, while Mary squealed with delight.

'He's got more lives than a cat,' Lettie declared. 'But it'll be good to have him back.'

'I'm sure it will,' Naomi said. However, as she moved on to the next patient she felt almost jealous of a man who inspired such loyalty in his friends.

As she thought about Hank she realized that she'd been worrying for nothing. Hank would have a complete recovery, resume his full practice and she would return to Lakeside with a clear conscience. Her time here would soon become a distant memory of what-might-have-beens.

Walter Davenport strode into Hank's ICU cubicle, a picture of authority in his gray suit and slicked-back hair, and Adam recognized him immediately.

'How's he doing?' Walter asked Adam over the faint blip of various monitors.

'Good.'

Walter nodded. 'He's a tough old bird. Always was.' He stuck out his hand. 'You must be Parker.'

Adam moved from his place at Hank's side to the foot of the bed in order to accept the older man's greeting. 'Yes. How did you know?'

'He's spoken of you often and always with high regard.'

Adam stared at the silent man in the bed. 'Hank's important to me, too.'

'I don't suppose he ever mentioned how much he enjoyed playing practical jokes in med school.'

Adam grinned. 'No.'

Walter nodded. 'He loved to sneak into the dean's office and dress up Harvey, the skeleton. Hank was always so imaginative. If a person lost anything—he never stole his costumes, mind you—he'd check with Harvey first.' He shook his head and grinned. 'Henry Taylor was—is—one of a kind.'

'He is,' Adam said fervently.

'How's Dr Stewart working out for you?'

The sudden change in subject caught Adam momentarily off guard. 'Couldn't be better.'

'Naomi's health is improving?'

Adam nodded. 'She looks better than she did a few weeks ago.'

'I was sorry to force her into a leave of absence but it was the only way she'd slow down long enough to recover. She has a tendency to make herself indispensable. Being a good doctor, it's easy to do.'

'Yes, it is.' Adam had seen several physicians give

of themselves to the point where they were totally worn out.

'We're trying to fill a shift supervisor position, as I'm sure you've heard.'

'Naomi's mentioned it.'

'The caliber of physicians who've applied has been excellent. It's been difficult to decide,' Walter said.

The perfect opportunity to keep Naomi in Deer Creek stared Adam in the face. All it would take were a few well-chosen phrases to tie Naomi's services in with the merger plans and Davenport wouldn't send her elsewhere.

Yet those words wouldn't come—he couldn't manipulate events to suit himself. At one time he would have done without a qualm, but not any more. He wouldn't be able to live with himself if he took away her fondest wish—he loved her too much to do that.

If Naomi stayed then she had to do so out of her own free will.

'If she's selected we'll be sorry to see her go.'

'Really?' Davenport's interest was palpable. 'She's met your expectations?'

'Definitely. I can't speak well enough of her or her abilities. She's done a marvelous job.'

'Then your medical staff is willing to proceed with our business arrangement?'

Temptation loomed ahead but he resisted it. 'If Naomi represents the caliber of doctor we can expect to cover our ER in the future we can't complain.'

Walter pressed his mouth into a line and wrinkled his brow in thought. Adam wished he knew what was on the man's mind. Still, he'd given Naomi a glowing recommendation which could only help her chances.

Naomi's fate—and his—rested in her superior's hands.

'You wouldn't object if I arranged for her permanent transfer to your facility?' Walter asked.

Suspecting a trap, Adam scrambled to extricate himself. 'No, but it should be her decision. If you toss her into a situation she doesn't want we'll both lose.'

Walter stroked his chin in thought. 'It's possible, I suppose. Still, one never knows. . .' He thrust out his hand. 'I appreciate your comments. Nice meeting you, Doctor.' He walked out with self-assured strides.

Adam was left with a sense of impending doom. Davenport's pointed questions suggested that Naomi's future had been arranged and only awaited Adam's confirmation. If she discovered the behind-the-scenes maneuvering she'd pack her bags and leave Deer Creek—and him—behind in a trail of dust.

A dark-haired nurse with the personality of a drill sergeant bustled in to check Hank's vital signs. 'Time's up. Dr Taylor needs his rest.'

Adam bent to whisper in Hank's ear. 'I'll be back in a day or two, ace. Hang in there.'

A small smile tugged at the corners of Hank's mouth and his eyelids fluttered open. 'Better believe it,' he managed to say, his voice faint. He clutched Adam's hand in a surprisingly firm grip. 'Walt means well. Has a tendency to. . .railroad people. Don't let him.'

Adam squeezed Hank's arm and strode out of ICU. He found his mother and Eloise in the waiting room. 'He's starting to come around but he'll be groggy for some time. Why don't you take a break? Someone will call or page us if there's any change.'

They agreed, and after Adam had settled them into

a guest room provided for family members of patients he headed for Deer Creek. For the next hour he pondered his course of action. Should he alert Naomi to Davenport's possible plans under the guise of forewarned was forearmed?

Yet what if he'd misread the situation? There was no point in fretting over a problem that didn't exist.

Within a few miles of his destination his cellular phone rang and he answered as he navigated the traffic.

'How's Hank?' Tyler Davis asked.

'Great,' Adam said. For the next few days he'd be asked that question often and he might as well get used to it.

'Good. I hate to bother you, but can you stop by my office?'

'Sure. I'll see you first thing in the morning.'

'I wouldn't wait that long.'

Adam was puzzled by his colleague's cryptic remarks. 'What's up?'

'I'd rather discuss it in private,' he said.

'OK. I should be there in a few minutes.'

'I'll be waiting.'

Naomi closed Dana Mitchell's chart and slid it into the bin for the secretary to file. 'The last patient for the day.'

'I thought we'd never finish, thanks to Morley Shields,' Mary declared. 'I've never heard him complain of so many ailments at once and they all seemed like textbook cases, too. How in the world did you ever get rid of him?'

Naomi smiled. 'I mentioned that with all of his problems we'd start with a bone marrow, followed by a spinal tap.'

'You didn't!' Mary giggled.

Naomi nodded. 'He seemed most interested until I showed him the needles and explained the procedures in great detail.' She gave a theatrical sigh. 'It was the most amazing thing. He experienced a miraculous recovery.'

'Come, ladies,' Lettie announced from the hallway. 'Let's lock up so I can go home. My grandson's playing a baseball game tonight and I want a good seat.'

'Go ahead,' Naomi said. 'I want to finish my notes on Mr Shields while they're still fresh. See you tomorrow.'

Mary, Lettie and the receptionist disappeared. When the door opened a few minutes later Naomi didn't glance up from the chart lying on the receptionist's desk. 'What did you forget?' she asked absent-mindedly.

'Not a thing,' Adam answered.

She glanced up and her welcoming smile came easily. 'You're back!'

'About an hour ago,' he admitted, sauntering through the doorway and into the clerical staff's office.

He looked weary, as if he had an unpleasant task ahead. Instantly, her first thoughts were of Hank. 'Is Hank OK?'

'He's fine. I've been meaning to ask, but never did. Has Rachel spoken with you about our charting requirements?'

'Yes, and I've made a point of dotting every i and crossing every t on every form available.'

'You're certain?'

'Absolutely. Is she still complaining?'

He ran his hands over his short hair. 'She's mentioned a lack of co-operation on your part.'

Naomi jammed her pen into her pocket, leaned back and folded her arms. 'I've done everything she's asked, and then some. From the very beginning, I might add.'

'Are you sure?'

'Absolutely.'

His face still appeared troubled. 'There's more, isn't there?' she guessed.

He gave an imperceptible nod. 'I've been asked to head an inquiry panel. It concerns you.'

Dread struck her heart. 'Oh?'

He nodded, his mouth set into a hard line. 'Mrs Lang is questioning her husband's death.'

CHAPTER NINE

'SHE'S accusing me of malpractice?' Naomi asked, frozen in horror at the words guaranteed to produce dread in any physician.

Adam fidgeted. 'Not in so many words. Apparently Mrs Lang has been hearing rumors from hospital personnel concerning her husband's care in the ER. She's requested an inquiry.'

'But she knew he was beyond help from the very beginning. She admitted it.'

He lifted one shoulder in a shrug. 'She's apparently having second thoughts.'

Naomi gave him a scathing glance and rose to pace. 'It was a clear-cut case of instantaneous death. Ask the paramedics who went to the house. Better yet, read the chart.'

'That's where the problem comes in. I found a few gaps you'll have to explain.'

'Gaps?'

To her consternation, he didn't go into detail. 'We'll also interview the staff involved.'

'I should hope so. Rich, Dale and Lacey will substantiate my decision to stop CPR.' She leaned against the desk. 'This makes absolutely no sense because I documented *everything*. Besides, it happened weeks ago. Why bring it up now?'

He shrugged. 'It's either hold an inquiry or Mrs Lang will press legal charges.'

'Regardless, my medical expertise is being questioned.' She scrutinized his face. 'Or are you afraid I made a judgemental error?'

'No.' He nearly shouted. 'I want this resolved with the least amount of fuss and hassle to everyone. Especially you.'

'That's some comfort.' She rubbed the back of her neck and straightened. 'When will you call the panel together?'

'Next week. I'll let you know as soon as we schedule a specific time to hear your testimony.'

More like grill me, she thought.

'For what it's worth, I don't think you made any errors. Other than your paperwork.'

She bristled. 'My paperwork *is*—or I should say *was*—in order. Perhaps you should have a chat with your medical records staff.' She pivoted to leave, but he grabbed her arm and swung her around.

'I'm trying to help you,' he said.

'Are you?' she asked quietly.

His face took on a wounded appearance. 'Do you really have to ask?'

She sighed. 'I don't know what to think any more.'

Adam stepped closer. 'Then don't. Just consider this.' He bent his head and kissed her.

'Naomi? What's happening?' Howard Shapiro's familiar husky voice came across the wire on the following Monday.

'Hi, Howard,' she answered, picturing her old classmate with his perpetually unkempt hair and clothes that—if it weren't for his wife—wouldn't match. 'I'm on my way to a medical staff meeting.'

'Then I won't keep you. Thought you'd want to know about the case you referred to me,' he said. 'A Lynda Akers.'

'What did you find?'

'It's a melanoma, all right. The lab report indicates a tumor thickness of approximately one millimeter. I removed a good margin of tissue so I'm sure we got it all.'

Naomi remembered how the least invasive conditions were given the best prognosis. Howard's report placed Lynda in the ninety to ninety-four per cent success range, as opposed to those where the tumor extended further into the dermis.

'What about radiation therapy?'

'I plan to start that as soon as possible. Luckily, her lymph nodes are clear.'

'Thanks for seeing her so quickly.'

'My pleasure. By the way, how are things in the boonies?'

She chuckled. 'Not bad.'

'Looking forward to coming back to civilization and practicing *real* medicine?'

His unflattering reference to Deer Creek bothered her more than she cared to admit. 'I suppose.'

'How much longer do you have?'

As tomorrow was the Fourth of July and the start of the Independence Day holiday weekend her answer came easily. 'Eight weeks. Give or take a few days.'

'Call when you get back. Marge and I will find a babysitter and we'll get theater tickets.'

'It's a date.' She replaced the receiver and dashed out of the ER to catch an unscheduled medical staff meeting. As she slid into a back row seat next to Adam she noticed a number of dignitaries at the front of the room, namely Deer Creek's chief executive officer, Lakeside's CEO and the two facilities' chiefs of staff, Dr Davis and Walter Davenport.

Something big was about to happen for this much brass to be in one place.

Michael Rosenberg, Deer Creek's representative, wearing his dress-for-success suit, lumbered to his feet and the expectant hum of the crowd died into complete silence.

'Thanks for taking time out of your schedules to attend this meeting. As you know, we've been hammering out an agreement between our two institutions for quite a while.'

Several physicians in the audience nodded.

'There have been major issues to resolve over the past few months, requiring give and take on both sides,' Rosenberg continued. He glanced at the men at the table. 'We've worked through those concerns at great length and reached what we feel is a suitable compromise. Hopefully, it's one you can live with.'

A huge smile appeared on the forty-nine-year-old Rosenberg's face and he beamed with delight. 'We've signed the papers and are now officially a sister institution to Lakeside Memorial Hospital.'

A round of applause shattered the quiet. After a few minutes Rosenberg lifted his hands for silence. 'We're prepared to answer your questions.'

'What about our ER coverage?'

Naomi strained her ears for Rosenberg's reply. Dr Davenport answered instead.

'Dr Stewart will continue until we make more permanent arrangements. We have someone in mind, but the details haven't been finalized yet. Effective August first we'll rotate our residents here to staff ER on the weekends, namely from Friday afternoon to Monday morning.'

'Can we expect a new ER physician every few months, like we've had in the past?'

Naomi didn't recognize the owner of the voice, although she craned her neck in the general vicinity.

'We hope to place a physician here who is interested in staying long-term. If the individual we have in mind turns down this position our recruiters will search for other candidates. To eliminate some of the past problems, your medical board will be actively involved in the selection process. Keep in mind, however, that this person will supervise our interns and residents as well so he or she must also meet our expectations.'

The questions posed faded into the background as Naomi wondered which of her fellow Lakeside physicians had volunteered to come to Deer Creek. She couldn't recall a single ER colleague who had ever mentioned a desire to relocate to a small community.

She tuned back in to the conversation to hear Rosenberg say, 'Thank you for coming.'

The doctors rose, some leaving and others meandering around the room to talk. Naomi edged her way to the front, intent on talking to Davenport.

She caught his attention and he strode forward, steering her into a quiet corner. 'Naomi. You're looking well.'

'Thank you. I'm feeling great, too.'

'For the record, this merger wouldn't have taken place without you. You've made a lot of people happy,' he said.

Naomi grinned at his praise.

'In fact, you'll have several nice recommendations in your personnel file. Not just from me, but from others as well.' He clapped his hand on her shoulder. 'Aren't you glad you stuck it out after all?'

She nodded. Her smile wavered as she thought of the upcoming inquiry, but she quickly shook off the worry. She'd followed the standards of care and acted as any other doctor would have done in a similar situation. There wasn't much she could have done anyway— Chester Lang had been beyond saving.

'Your success was definitely considered when we selected our ER supervisor.'

A tremor of excitement ran down her spine. Her dreams were about to be fulfilled. 'Then you've decided.'

Davenport nodded. 'With the large number of well-qualified applicants, we didn't see a reason to delay.'

Naomi's pager beeped with a message to return to the emergency room. For once she found the interruption irritating.

'Obviously now isn't the time to discuss your future,' Walter said with a smile. 'I'll be in Deer Creek for most of the day. We'll visit before I leave.'

'I'm looking forward to it.' As she slipped past the thinning crowd her heart swelled with elation. Her promotion was a sure thing—she sensed it.

'I wish the city would ban individual fireworks,' Lacey grumbled. 'There's another kid in room two with burns from a sparkler.'

'Starting early, aren't they? I thought Deer Creek had

a local ordinance prohibiting use except on the holiday itself,' Naomi said.

'We do, but some people don't pay attention.'

'How typical.' Naomi walked into the room to find eight-year-old Charlie and his mother.

'Let's have a look,' she said. 'Does it hurt?'

Charlie nodded, his face tear-stained and smudged with dirt.

Naomi studied the scattered burns on the back of Charlie's hands, which didn't seem to be serious, and the long angry mark across one thigh, which was red and blistering. 'What happened?'

'I was holding a sparkler but the sparks jumped on me. It hurt and when I dropped it it fell against my leg.'

His mother broke in. 'I cooled his skin with water, like the newspaper said in the article about firework safety. But his leg looked awful so I brought him here.'

'Sparklers can get as hot as twelve hundred degrees Fahrenheit,' Naomi said. 'The burn is rather deep and he'll probably have a scar. Fortunately, it isn't on his face.

'We'll use an antibiotic on the burned area and cover it with a loose dressing so keep it clean and dry. Are his immunizations current?'

His mother nodded.

'After Lacey is finished you may leave. Bring him to my office on Monday so I can see how he's doing.'

She carried Charlie's notes to the nurses' station, and as she jotted down her recommendations she wondered when she'd begun to think of Adam's office as hers.

Lacey hung up the telephone. 'You don't have to stay. Kirby is on call.'

Naomi picked up the next clipboard and scanned the

symptoms Lacey had jotted down. 'Since Adam closed the office for the holiday I told Kirby I'd cover for him.'

'Why did you do that?'

'He should spend the day with his family. As I don't have any kids to worry about. . .' Her voice faded.

Lacey shook her head. 'You're too soft-hearted. The doctors will take advantage of you.'

'With Hank still in the hospital, I'd spend the day rattling around the house by myself. I'd rather be here than sitting in front of the television watching Hank's library of John Wayne videos.'

'Do I detect a note of dislike toward Hank's collection?' Adam interrupted from behind. 'How un-American.'

Recognizing his voice, Naomi swung around. Her heart skipped a beat at his unexpected appearance, and she marveled at how his casual chinos and purple golf shirt suited him far better than a stuffy suit.

'They're OK, but I can't handle westerns and war movies as a steady diet. What are you doing here?'

'Same thing you are. I finished my rounds and decided I was thirsty. How about a Coke?'

'I was hoping someone would offer one,' she answered, 'but there are a few patients waiting—'

'Which I can handle,' Lacey insisted. 'Go on.'

Naomi quickly made her decision. 'Page me if you need me,' she instructed Lacey on her way out of the department.

'Have you talked to Walter Davenport?'

'Not at any great lengths, but he mentioned discussing my future.'

'Then you've decided against Deer Creek?'

'Hank is doing well. You don't need me.' Tell me

that *you* do, she silently begged. His affirmation would make all the difference. But he didn't say what she wanted to hear.

'Hank is contemplating retirement.'

She stopped in her tracks. 'There's no physical reason, is there?'

Adam shrugged. 'He says he wants to enjoy life. Fill in as a locum here and there, setting his own hours and his own pace.'

Before she could comment again Rachel Parker dashed down the corridor toward them, her soft-soled shoes making dull thuds against the linoleum. Her eyes were wide and her expression stunned.

The older woman rushed to Adam's side and gripped his arm. 'Tell me it isn't true,' she exclaimed, her breath short as if she'd been running.

'What isn't true?' he asked.

'The merger has been finalized. One of the ladies from Accounting just called with the news.'

'It's official,' he agreed. 'Everything's signed, sealed and delivered.'

'Oh, no.' Rachel shook her head and sank into one of the waiting room chairs.

'What's wrong?'

'All of my hard work was for nothing.' Rachel held her head in her hands.

Adam stared at Naomi. She shrugged. 'What are you talking about?' he asked.

'I tried to stop it. I did everything I could.'

'Tell me exactly what you've done.' Adam's voice was firm and full of authority.

'I didn't want Lakeside to buy us,' she said with defiance. 'The idea was a slap in the face of my father's memory. He struggled to make this a reputable hospital and now a huge organization wants to capitalize on his hard work. Your grandfather would roll over in his grave if he knew you'd allowed this.'

'The board of trustees made the decision. Besides, this action was meant to benefit the people of this community, Rachel. Grandad would have been pleased.'

Rachel visibly bristled and her eyes shot pure venom. 'I don't think he'd be happy to have incompetent physicians on staff.'

Suspicion grew in Naomi's mind but she held her counsel. This was Adam's relative and Adam needed to handle the situation.

His eyes narrowed. 'What have you done?' he repeated.

'I didn't want Lakeside to take us over. After they assigned those two inept physicians to us and you convinced the doctors to think twice about agreeing I thought everything was under control. But then *she*—' Rachel glared at Naomi '—came.'

'And?' Adam prompted.

'You were getting along too well so I took matters into my own hands.' Her shoulders slumped. 'Since you're a stickler for detail I misplaced Dr Stewart's records on a number of her patients so it would appear as if she wasn't doing her job.'

He looked stunned. 'Did you start the rumors about Chester Lang, too?'

Rachel looked away, but not before Naomi saw that her eyes were bright with tears. 'If an inquiry board investigated his death they'd see the shoddy documentation and would assume Dr Stewart isn't any more competent than her predecessors. It would be the proverbial last straw and negotiations would end.'

She rested her head in her hands. 'Now it doesn't matter. We're part of that. . .that overgrown health-care machine.'

Adam pinched the bridge of his nose. 'You've made a horrible mistake, Rachel. You, of all people, know the repercussions of falsifying records—those are legal documents.'

'I was trying to *save* our hospital,' she said defensively.

'The reasons don't matter. With everyone screaming for health-care reform, we needed to affiliate ourselves with a larger institution. Small places have a hard time staying afloat right now.' His tone became cold. 'What's unforgivable is how you tried to ruin a physician's reputation.'

She started to protest and he held up his hands to forestall her. 'The ends don't justify the means. For your own sake, it's time you retired.'

Rachel straightened. 'I suppose so,' she said wearily. 'But I couldn't let my father's memory die.'

'It won't,' Adam said. He turned to Naomi, his expression apologetic. 'Would you excuse me while I try to contain the damage?'

'Of course.' Naomi watched Adam escort his aunt toward the hospital entrance, glad that the case of the missing records had been solved but sorry that Adam's relative had caused the problem.

'Back so soon?' Lacey asked the minute Naomi stepped foot into the ER foyer.

'Afraid so. Adam ran into a situation that couldn't wait.' Although Lacey was part of the family the news of Rachel's activities should come from Adam, not herself.

Naomi peered at the next clipboard. 'Anything interesting?'

'A bee sting, a sprained ankle and a kid who lives to shove things up his nose. This time it's a jelly bean. Anyway, take your pick.'

'The jelly bean sounds like fun,' she said facetiously. 'I'll take him first.'

Lacey motioned down the hallway. 'Room two.'

For the next few hours Naomi was kept busy with a host of minor complaints. Unfortunately, the cases didn't demand her full attention and her thoughts returned to Davenport's conversation.

Immense satisfaction filled her soul—her hard work had paid off. With this promotion, she was on a steady climb to success—a climb that had started with medical school, then progressed to being selected as senior ER resident and now this. If she continued to work hard— and this promotion guaranteed long hours—who knew what would be the next rung on her way to the top?

Suddenly she felt a new sympathy for Cynthia. Adam would certainly feel betrayed and utterly rejected if Naomi placed her career first as Cynthia had.

Adam's smiling face appeared in her mind's eye and her excitement deflated. Until she'd met him her profession had been *the* most important thing in her life. Now, however, it wasn't.

Yet what choice did she have? He'd never spoken of love or suggested a future other than to step into Hank's shoes. The chemistry was there but, after watching his relationship with his siblings, she was certain he wanted someone who'd lean on him—who couldn't make a decision without his input.

She was far too independent. Her love couldn't flourish under those conditions. Before she knew it he'd leave, just like her father had abandoned her mother.

No, if Davenport offered her the job she'd take it.

Having strengthened her resolve, she expected to feel at peace. Surprisingly enough, she didn't. Mulling over the reason, she took time to check on Edith Stone.

'Your test results are much better,' she said. 'Not normal, but you've shown a significant improvement these past few days.'

'Then you'll release me?'

Edith's excitement brought a smile to Naomi's mouth. 'We'll monitor your coagulation times on an outpatient basis. Has the counselor been in?'

'We've had a wonderful chat,' Edith declared. 'Even though Dean has left me I know I can cope.'

The older woman's confidence was palpable and Naomi's reservations faded. 'I'm glad to hear it. I'll sign the forms so you can go home as soon as you're ready.'

To Naomi's amusement, Edith jumped out of bed before she'd finished her sentence.

After writing new orders and scrawling her signature on the proper forms, Naomi returned to her department. As she pushed the swinging doors open Lacey looked up. 'Cancel the page. She's just come in.'

'What's up?' Naomi asked.

'We just got a call on the scanner. There's been a boating accident at the lake.'

'Any injuries?'

'No one knows for sure. A sailboat overturned. Someone's in the water and a rescue unit's trying to fish him out. The trauma room's ready.'

'Hopefully, it's only a minor mishap and the sailor was wearing a life jacket.'

A few minutes later the radio crackled to life. Naomi grabbed the handset. 'Go ahead, unit two.'

'We have a near-drowning victim in his early fifties,' the paramedic reported. 'He is conscious and has spontaneous respiration, although he's complaining of chest pain. We're administering oxygen and have immobilized the cervical spine.'

Naomi depressed the button so that the rescue team could hear her. 'That's a fresh-water lake, isn't it?'

'Affirmative.'

'Start an IV with five per cent dextrose in water,' Naomi ordered. 'Transport as soon as possible.'

'Ten-four,' came the reply as her orders were acknowledged.

'As soon as he's here I want a urinalysis, CBC, electrolytes and blood gases, along with c-spine and chest X-rays. Oh, and don't forget an EKG and warm blankets for hypothermia.'

Lacey hurried to make preparations, and ten minutes later the ambulance pulled into the driveway. Dale and Rich unloaded their passenger, Ted Abrams.

'He wasn't in the water for more than a few minutes,' Dale reported. 'A bystander dived in after him and nearly had him to shore by the time we arrived.'

'How're you doing, Ted?' Naomi asked.

Ted grimaced. 'Not too bad. Swallowed half the lake, I did.'

'Were you drinking any alcohol?'

'Not a drop. Only soda pop.'

At least she didn't have to deal with alcohol intoxication. Naomi listened to his chest and heard the distinctive wheezing. The nail beds of his fingers were tinged with blue, indicating a cyanosis, and his heart rate was fast.

Mentally she prepared for the worst—cardiac arrest or pulmonary failure, to name but two. After those dangers had passed the slower complications could develop—things like pulmonary edema and convulsions.

Once again it occurred to her that if this same scenario occurred at Lakeside—and it had—she would send Mr Abrams upstairs and into the care of another doctor. She'd never know how he was doing unless word filtered down or she made a point of finding out.

Now, however, she would see him through to the end—preferably to a full recovery—and she was glad. If nothing else, her stint had changed her into a more caring doctor, one who could look at the whole person and not merely as a body part to be repaired and sent on.

For the first time in her career she wondered if she'd be as satisfied with Emergency Room duty as she had in the past.

'Lab results are here,' Lacey announced, breaking into Naomi's musing.

'Thanks.' She scanned the reports. The chest and cervical spine X-rays looked normal, the EKG showed a slightly irregular heartbeat and the blood tests were within the reference ranges. Abrams's oxygen saturation levels were slightly low but not critical. In all, he was in better shape than she'd anticipated, and she was happy to report her findings both to her patient and to his recently arrived wife.

'I'm going to admit you for observation,' Naomi said. 'Right now you're in good shape, but you're not totally risk-free.'

'I'm not? I thought that since I was still breathing I was fine.' He chuckled and winked at his wife who appeared greatly relieved by Naomi's news.

Naomi smiled. 'Your body has had a shock and will be trying to compensate. We'll monitor you for twenty-four to forty-eight hours for any developing problems with your heart, brain or lungs. There's also the risk of infection from all the dirty water.'

'I guess. You're the expert.' His eyes narrowed. 'I won't have to eat stuff like broth and gelatin, will I?'

Naomi studied his large girth. 'We won't let you starve.'

'Huh,' he grumbled without malice.

Naomi strode out of the room and minutes later a nurse and an aide arrived to wheel Mr Abrams to a bed in Intensive Care. For the first time in several hours the department was quiet.

'Do you suppose it's safe for me to go home?' Naomi joked.

'I'll keep it quiet for you,' Lacey promised. 'At least until my shift ends in thirty minutes.'

'Gee, thanks.'

Suddenly Lacey glanced toward the door. 'Sorry. Looks like you can't leave yet. Another customer.'

Naomi turned and recognized Walter Davenport. Her stomach danced with anticipation. 'No, he's from Lakeside.' She strode toward him, wearing a welcoming smile. 'I was afraid I'd missed you.'

'Had some last-minute details to work out. Is there a place we can talk privately?'

Naomi led him to one of the exam rooms. 'Is this OK?'

'Fine.' He closed the door and drew a deep breath.

Her heart pounded and each second until he spoke seemed like hours.

'There's no way to soften this so I won't. We've selected Anthony Delacourte to fill the ER supervisor position at Lakeside.'

CHAPTER TEN

NAOMI'S world shattered into a million pieces. 'Anthony Delacourte?' she parroted.

'I know this comes as a surprise—'

'I'll say.' Tony was a nice man and an excellent diagnostician, but he'd always seemed content with his staff physician status. He was someone who kept his own counsel and she couldn't remember a time when he'd mentioned higher aspirations, although obviously he must have had them.

'Anthony is a stable family man who will do a fine job.'

Frustration tugged at her spirits. The very thing she'd shunned in order to advance her career had obviously been her downfall.

'Not only has he been at Lakeside for a long time, but he's acted as the department head these past few months. Done well, too.'

'I see.' She forced all emotion off her face, railing at the fates for an illness at the most inopportune time in her life.

'As I said earlier, I'd like to discuss your future.'

Naomi steeled herself for another shock.

'You've done such an excellent job here that we'd like to offer you the full-time ER position.'

She swallowed hard.

'We considered a permanent transfer after Dr Parker spoke so highly of you—'

167

'He what?' Interrupting her superior was not her usual practice, but she wasn't concerned about etiquette at the moment. Her eyes narrowed. 'When?'

'I visited with Adam about a week ago. He's impressed with you and your work. In fact, he appeared quite taken with you.' He looked pleased with himself.

Anger burst into flame. Did Adam's controlling arm extend to everyone and not just members of his own family? No wonder his sisters tested the limits at every turn.

'He said that?' she ground out.

Walter shook his head. 'Not in so many words, but our brief meeting was most informative. Dr Parker has a lot of good ideas.'

I'm sure, she thought unreasonably, certain that Adam had influenced Davenport in a way that benefited Adam Parker. 'You said something about a permanent transfer?'

'That was our original plan.'

Naomi stood ramrod-stiff and crossed her arms. 'Then it's settled? I'm supposed to stay here?'

Walter's eyes widened as if he was surprised. 'You don't want to?'

'No.' Not if Adam will manipulate my life to suit his purposes, she silently added.

'I've thought long and hard over this situation,' he said. 'Based on my conversation with Adam, I tried to arrive at a mutually beneficial solution for everyone. If, however, you don't want the Deer Creek position then your job at Lakeside is still available.'

Davenport hadn't replaced her, she thought with relief.

'Although, if I were you, I'd seriously consider the

opportunities here.' He moved to the door. 'Take your time thinking it over.'

She nodded. For a few minutes after he'd left she sat in stunned silence as an ache settled into her chest. Adam had betrayed her and now she felt empty. A brisk knock broke through her numb state.

Lacey stuck her head in the door, then came in and closed it behind her. 'Bad news?'

Naomi managed a wan smile. 'I didn't get the promotion.'

Lacey sat next to her. 'I'm sorry.'

Naomi dug her hands in her pockets and fingered her fifty-cent piece. She wanted to reveal Adam's underhanded tactics but the pain was still too great and she couldn't. 'So am I.'

'What will you do?'

She took a moment to consider. Regardless of Anthony's character flaws, he *was* an excellent physician and she got along well with him. Working together wouldn't pose a major problem and she would soon settle into her old routine.

But did she want her old routine?

Frustrated and angered by Adam's machinations, she stood by her earlier decision. 'I'm going back to Kansas City.'

'Honestly, Adam,' Lacey began as soon as she tracked him down at his home the next day, 'Naomi was absolutely devastated. I've never seen a person look as crushed as she did.'

'I can't blame her, can you?' Adam said, pacing the floor of his kitchen. 'She's been working toward this her entire life.'

'She's going back to Kansas City.'

His worst fears were coming true—she obviously didn't want him or Hank's practice. He pressed his mouth into a hard line.

'The thing is, I just don't understand why. Her decision doesn't make sense.'

It did to him. 'Maybe she's more like Cynthia than you thought.'

'I don't believe that.'

Neither did Adam, but if she'd truly wanted to stay in Deer Creek—with him—the loss of her promotion should have helped her make the decision in his favor. Since it hadn't. . .

Lacey placed her hands on her hips. 'I can't believe you're so laid-back about this.'

'What do you want me to do?'

'I don't know. Any other time you'd be on the phone, making personal contacts, calling in favors—*any-thing*—to get what you want.'

'For your information,' he said, running his hand over his hair and allowing his impatience to show, 'it's taking everything I have to keep from it.'

'Then why are you? Don't you *want* Naomi to stay?' Her dark eyes searched his face.

'Of course I do. I'm only following your advice.'

She rolled her eyes heavenward. 'That's a first. Too bad I can't remember what sage words of wisdom I might have given my brother that he actually took to heart.'

He paused for a fraction of a second. 'It has to be her decision,' he said quietly. 'No interference.'

Lacey studied him for a moment and Adam, for the first time he could remember, sensed that his sister saw the pain he'd been hiding over the prospect of Naomi's leaving.

'Does she know how you feel?' Lacey's tone was as soft as her touch on his arm.

'I tried to tell her,' he said, remembering how the sparks had flown in his bedroom, 'but, knowing how career-minded she is, I tried to approach the subject of a future in our town from a business angle.'

'Honestly, Adam, you don't know anything about women, do you? You have to appeal to her softer side. Wine and dine and all that.'

'I promised not to pressure her into a decision.'

'You're kidding.' Lacey was incredulous.

He shook his head. 'Those tactics didn't work with Cynthia. I won't make the same mistake with Naomi.'

'Well, brother, dear, I hope this is one promise you won't regret.'

'So do I.'

The next evening, Naomi sat on Hank's deck in the dark with her hair loose, hardly noticing the city's colorful fireworks display fill the night sky. Lost in thought, she paid scant attention to the distant booms and the snap, crackle and whistles of the closer show, conducted by the neighborhood children.

'I wasn't sure you were home,' Adam said from the gate. 'At least, not until I saw the candle burning.'

She wanted to scream that she wasn't home, that this was Hank's house and she was only a temporary guest, but she didn't. Besides, she wasn't sure she had a place to call home. She had an apartment but, considering how much time she spent there, it was only a place to change clothes and grab a few winks of sleep.

'Yeah, well, here I am.'

'Watching the fireworks?' he asked.

'Sort of.'

'Mind if I watch with you?'

'As a matter of fact, I do.'

The gate squeaked in the darkness and footsteps thudded against the flagstones. By the time his familiar face appeared above the deck railing his feet were pounding on the wooden stairs. The cushion creaked as he settled into the chair opposite hers.

'Remind me to have Lacey buy you a hearing-aid for your birthday,' she said tartly. 'When is it, anyway?'

'Twenty-fourth of March. You obviously don't know about a rule we have in Deer Creek.'

'Which is?'

'No one's allowed to be alone on the Fourth of July.'

She sent a glare in his direction. 'Yeah, right.'

He glanced at the sky. 'Nice night.'

She answered with silence.

'I talked to Lacey this morning. I'm sorry they didn't offer you the promotion.'

Her throat burned. 'Me, too.'

'Lacey tells me you're going back to Kansas City, anyway.'

'I can't work with people who take matters into their own hands to suit themselves.'

'What are you talking about?'

'Your chat with Davenport.' Her tone was sharp. 'Or have you forgotten?'

'He asked me how things were working out. I complimented you by saying how much we enjoyed having you on staff.'

She narrowed her eyes, his form illuminated only by

the glowing citronella candle which served to ward off the bugs. 'Knowing how you dictate to your sisters, are you certain that your so-called compliment didn't come out as a demand?'

He bristled. 'Is that what you think? That I convinced Davenport to pass you over so you'd stay here?' Sounding incredulous, he shook his head. 'I didn't realize my persuasive powers were so extensive.'

She blinked away the moisture in her eyes. 'You said you wouldn't pressure me and, instead, you pressured Walter.'

'I apologize if he took my praise for your abilities the wrong way.'

'If that's supposed to make me feel better it isn't working.' She paused. 'I trusted you, Adam. I trusted you to stick to your word. You had no right to interfere in my life, and you did.'

He sat on the edge of the chair, his hands clenched between his knees. 'I don't know Walter very well but he strikes me as a man who does what he wants, whenever he wants, regardless of anyone's input.'

She fell silent. Adam's comment held an undeniable truth but she couldn't admit it. She wasn't ready to let go of her anger. 'The facts remain. You took the decision out of my hands.'

'The choice you face is slightly different,' he said, 'but, regardless of the actual job, it still boils down to Deer Creek versus Lakeside—that part hasn't changed. I'm curious, though. If Walter *had* offered you the position would you have accepted?'

Only because you don't love me, she screamed inside. Even now, she wanted him to ask her—no, beg her—to choose in his favor, to tell her those precious words.

To her disappointment he didn't and she struggled to hide the pain that was piercing her heart.

'I'd considered turning him down,' she admitted, 'but I've seen you in action. You want people dependent on you and I won't become something I'm not.'

A cricket chirped in the silence and the last of the fireworks disappeared.

He rose. Before he spoke she knew that she'd hurt him terribly. 'If that's what you think,' he ground out, 'then there's no point in my being here.'

His feet stomped across the wooden deck and down the stairs. She jumped up. 'Adam, wait.'

The gate slammed in reply. She sank onto the top step, and tears rolled down her face.

'Naomi! I wasn't expecting you for several hours yet.' A smile wreathed Hank's face as he sat against the pillows on his hospital bed.

She placed the book and spectacles on the nightstand and leaned over to plant a kiss on his forehead. 'When you telephoned, asking for Tom Clancy's latest novel and your glasses, I thought you wanted them pronto.'

Hank's call had been a saving grace. The past few days since her confrontation with Adam had been unbearable. He rarely talked to her and when he did he stared right through her.

'You must be feeling much better,' she said, covering up her inner turmoil with a bright smile. 'It's good to see you looking so chipper.'

He grinned. 'The prospect of going home always perks up a patient's morale. You know that.'

'When will Melissa spring you from this joint?' she

teased. 'She's dying for any excuse to take a trip with her new car.'

'Tomorrow.'

Then why had he requested a book that he hadn't started yet? She sat in the chair next to his bed. 'I'm glad.'

'Adam tells me there's been a lot happening lately.'

'There has been,' she admitted. 'Who would have guessed that life in Deer Creek is as exciting as a daytime drama?'

'I've heard about Rachel. I'd never dreamed she'd become so upset by the two hospitals merging.'

'She's very loyal to her family, which is admirable. I'm thankful everything's been settled.' After the hospital authorities and Mrs Lang had heard Rachel's confession all hints of impropriety on Naomi's part had been dismissed.

'Walter told me about the promotion. I'm sorry it didn't work out for you.'

'Yeah, well, I suppose it's for the best.'

'He also mentioned you're returning to Lakeside.'

'For the time being.'

His eyes became intent. 'You can't adjust to living in our little community?'

'Deer Creek is a quaint town but there are other considerations.'

'Like what?'

She fussed with a wrinkle in his sheet. 'It's a family town, and with my track record of dysfunctional relationships I don't fit in.'

'Says who? If you and Adam have something going—'

'We don't.'

Hank struggled with the pillow behind his head and Naomi rushed to his aid. Once he'd leaned back he asked, 'Why not?'

She examined her fingernails. 'We're not compatible.'

Hank waved aside her remark.

'We argued.'

'Couples do that. Making up is the fun part.'

Naomi shook her head and gave him a half-smile. 'He's a special man, but he has such a strong tendency to control situations. Look at his family.' She warmed to her subject and met Hank's gaze. 'His sisters can't make a move without his approval. I can't function under those conditions.'

'That could be a problem,' Hank admitted.

'It's a *major* problem,' she corrected. 'He's already interfered with my life. He told Dr Davenport he wanted me in Deer Creek and, next thing I knew, someone else got the job I'd thought was mine.'

Hank stroked his whiskery chin. 'It may look that way, but I've known Walter for years and I know how he operates. When he asked Adam if he wanted you to stay in Deer Creek Walt already had his mind made up.'

'You really think so?'

'I was a little muddled at the time but I caught most of the conversation. Didn't Adam explain?'

Naomi was sure that her face had turned a bright shade of pink. 'I didn't believe him. I guess I let my perceptions of his relationship with his sisters blind me to the truth.'

'I'll admit he keeps close tabs on the girls, but have you looked at his motives?'

'N-o-o,' she said slowly.

'Some people control others because of the feeling of power it gives them. Others do it out of love. Granted, there is a fine line but can you honestly say that Adam prevents them from being independent?'

She thought for a moment. While Adam dispensed advice freely he also did it in such a manner as to provoke them into considering all the angles of the situation.

'No,' she said slowly.

'You see?' Hank sounded triumphant. 'Actually, you and Adam aren't very different.'

Naomi's jaw dropped. 'You're joking.'

'No, I'm not. You're both afraid of losing someone but you react to your fear in opposite ways. While you keep your distance Adam pulls people closer.'

Could Hank be right? Even as she asked herself the question, she recognized the truth. Adam had mentioned at the hospital picnic how he felt compelled to curb his sisters' impulsiveness to save his mother grief; it was his way of holding his family together. How could she have forgotten—or misread him? The thought pained her.

Hank yawned and his eyelids drifted shut. Mindful of his need for rest, Naomi rose to plant a goodbye kiss against his sunken cheek. 'Thanks for everything, Hank,' she murmured. 'I'll see you at home tomorrow.'

He clutched her hand without opening his eyes. 'Don't forget what I told you.'

'I won't.'

She tiptoed from the room, closing the door behind her with a quiet click. Her steps led her to the elevator and she got in. Without thinking, she followed a route she'd made countless times—the route to Emergency Services.

Along the way she breathed in the scent of disinfectant, of alcohol, of fear and of death. She stood on the threshold of her old department, surveying the organized chaos that stretched out before her. Her muscles tensed and the familiar rush of adrenalin surged through her.

She missed this place.

She walked through the hallways and peered into cubicles full of people, heard the low murmur of voices and an occasional call to an orderly down the hall. Babies cried, toddlers whimpered and adults sat in the waiting room in stony silence, awaiting their turn to have their particular pain eased.

She didn't recognize a single patient's face or know a single patient's identity which—oddly enough, after her stint at Deer Creek—seemed strange.

A voice called out her name. She turned toward the voice and saw Marjie Henson, the forty-year-old nurse responsible for bringing order out of confusion.

'Dr Stewart! It's good to see you. Are you ready to join the rat race again?' Marjie teased.

'I'm feeling much better,' Naomi replied, sidestepping the question. 'Thanks for asking.'

Marjie stopped a young Hispanic orderly and handed him the chart she'd been carrying. 'If X-Ray hasn't come for Five B go park her on their doorstep. We need the space.'

The young man nodded and set off.

'Busy place,' Naomi remarked.

'As always. We've got everything from a possible

concussion to a broken foot.' Marjie grinned. 'Never a dull moment.'

The automatic doors whooshed open and paramedics raced in with a gurney, followed by several policemen. 'Gotta run,' Marjie said as she rushed forward with two other nurses and a doctor Naomi had never seen before.

She stepped aside to allow the party to pass, over-hearing the paramedic's report as they pushed the patient into the nearest available trauma room. 'Male, age seventeen. Multiple stab wounds. At least six.'

From the amount of blood covering the youth, the size of the knife sticking out of his chest and the vital signs recited time was of the essence. She was ready to offer her services when another resident rushed in.

Feeling extraneous but unable to leave, she remained in the background. Doctors' orders filled the air—orders for crossmatches and IVs and a host of other life-saving measures, while nurses rushed to do their bidding.

'Get him up to surgery, stat,' someone said.

In the next heartbeat the EKG line went flat and all the team's effort to revive him failed. Latex gloves snapped and the yellow disposable gowns crinkled as the two doctors pulled the protective gear off their bodies and stuffed the items into the trash can.

The paramedics left soon after, their steps slow and weary and their faces etched with the disappointment that came from knowing that death had won this battle. She stopped one.

'What was his name?' she asked.

The man in his late twenties, with eyes as old as time, shrugged. 'He was alone when we found him. No ID.'

'Oh.' Intense sorrow pierced her. It would be hours, perhaps days, before the young man's family—if he even had one—would learn of his death.

She missed Deer Creek.

At that moment she knew that she couldn't return to Lakeside and its impersonal atmosphere. She'd outgrown her desire to keep people at a distance. Adam's methods might need some balance but they seemed infinitely superior to hers.

Naomi glanced across the rows of chairs, her gaze landing on a young couple in their early twenties, holding hands.

Immediately she thought of Adam. She'd wanted him to sweep her off her feet, profess undying love, propose marriage—say *something* to give her a clear picture of what he wanted from her.

No pressure, he'd said, and he'd kept his word. But if he truly cared about her wouldn't he have made it plain? Or had the prospect of marriage to someone from a poor background made him cautious?

A woman, dressed in a chic suit with diamonds dripping from her hands, strode toward the nurses' station and Naomi had her answer.

Her upbringing hadn't been a factor. Adam was afraid—afraid of repeating his history with Cynthia, afraid of Naomi's rejection. And, if she was right, no wonder he didn't tell her of his love or spend his time convincing her to stay.

His no-pressure policy made sense. Adam Parker, for all his bark, had fears like everyone else.

Her future plans became as clear as purified water, the right fork in the road as noticeable as if it were illuminated by a neon signpost. The prospect of a promotion had clouded her vision but, as Adam had said, her choice lay between Deer Creek and Lakeside. Nothing more, nothing less.

She jumped to her feet and hurried toward the main part of the hospital. Brushing past people in the corridor, she was thankful for Hank's smokescreen request because it provided her with the opportunity to see her job at Lakeside for what it was, not what she'd imagined it to be.

In less than an hour Naomi was on the highway with a precious envelope in her purse. She made the drive to Deer Creek in record time, pushing the speed limit to the maximum in her haste to find Adam and clear the air. By the time she arrived it was nearly six o'clock.

Adam's Jeep was missing from his driveway and she took a chance that he was at the hospital. His vehicle was in the doctors' parking lot and she pulled into the space beside his, brakes squealing.

'Where's Dr Parker?' she asked at the desk a few minutes later in a breathless tone.

'In Emergency,' the receptionist replied.

Naomi rushed to the ER. To her surprise, Lacey was on duty. 'Is Adam here?'

The nurse nodded. 'He's in the lounge with *that* woman.' She grimaced.

Naomi stopped short. 'What woman?'

'Cynthia St John, that's who.'

Dread replaced Naomi's high spirits. '*The* Cynthia St John?'

'None other. She drove into town and had a flat tire. George from the service station dropped her off here as Adam wasn't at home. Speaking of which, you're home early. How's Hank?'

'Fine. You can pass the information along to Adam when you see him.'

Lacey came around the desk. 'Tell him yourself.'

'I can't. . .' Having had his cold fury directed toward her, she couldn't stand seeing him give Cynthia one of his knee-weakening smiles.

'You may not be able to, but I can.' Lacey grabbed her arm to pull her along. Once they reached the staff lounge Lacey released her arm and Naomi took a deep breath. Before she could take a step over the threshold a feminine voice drifted out of the room.

'Adam, you were so right. Family is more important than a career.'

'It took you long enough to realize it,' he replied.

'I'm going to do things differently this time. I suppose I had to leave in order to discover what I really wanted.'

There was a noticeable pause, as if the two shared an embrace.

Naomi stared at Lacey. The nurse's face mirrored the dismay and horror Naomi felt.

She'd made her decision too late. Her window of opportunity had closed. Adam had already replaced her.

Naomi stiffened her spine, straightened her shoulders and race-walked toward the closest exit.

Lacey followed. 'You're not going to leave her with him, are you?'

'Watch me.'

Ignoring Lacey's protests, Naomi forced herself to a normal pace as she headed for the parking lot. With a death-like grip on the steering-wheel, she drove to Hank's house and parked inside the dark garage.

She'd been so excited coming home, confident that she could tell Adam about her self-discovery and make amends. But Cynthia had obviously made the same discovery and now Naomi didn't have a chance.

The inside of the house was cool and welcoming, but Naomi paid little attention as she yanked the envelope from her purse. Its contents were useless now. She tossed it on the coffee-table with the other junk mail destined for the trash and dropped her purse on the recliner, before sinking onto the sofa.

Miserably she stretched out, flinging one arm over her burning eyes.

No matter how anxious Adam might be for her to leave, she wouldn't until she'd fulfilled her commitment to Hank. Having had a taste of a different, more personalized working environment, she couldn't return to Lakeside either. Beth and Tristan had often tried to lure her to their hometown of Mercer. It, too, was small like Deer Creek—maybe now was the time to accept their invitation.

Adam strode into Hank's house through the back-yard entrance as the front door was locked. Perhaps he should have called first, but if Naomi was in the same state of mind as Lacey she'd hang up on him as soon as she heard his voice.

He needed the advantage of surprise.

The house was silent, much like the last time he'd come through unannounced. Catching a whiff of Naomi's perfume, he peeked into the living room and saw her curled up on the sofa.

He approached her and paused within an arm's reach, glad for the carpeting's muffling qualities. She had flung one arm outward, her long braid falling over one shoulder to drape itself across her breast. Intense emotion pierced his chest and he prayed for the strength to tell her what had to be said.

He crouched down next to the coffee-table, ready to touch her shoulder—to feel her soft skin, her small bones—but out of the corner of one eye he saw an envelope on the table—a white envelope with his name in her bold, flowing script.

Trepidation came over him. He rose, snatched the letter from its place and ripped the glued flap open.

The sound of paper ripping brought Naomi out of her doze. While Adam unfolded the page inside she jerked herself upright, ready to snatch the form from his hands. 'You can't have that.'

He held the paper aloft. 'The envelope was addressed to me. That makes it mine.'

'I filled it out and I want it back.'

Adam scanned the paper. 'Does this mean what I think it means?'

'Not any more. I changed my mind.'

'Too bad because I won't let you.'

'What?' Her eyes widened.

'I won't let you change your mind,' he repeated.

She shook her head. 'Wait a minute. What about Cynthia?'

'Lacey repeated the part of the conversation you two overheard and, believe me, my ears will never be the same,' he said drily. 'For your information, Cynthia is getting married and she dropped by to tell me.'

'Then she's not moving back?'

He smiled. 'No.'

Sudden relief brought tears to her eyes.

He stroked the side of her face. 'Do you remember the night we watched the fireworks?'

She nodded slowly, warily.

'I wanted to tell you how much I loved you, but I couldn't. I justified my actions with all sorts of reasons—excuses, actually—I didn't want to pressure you; I wanted you to make the decision. Those were all true, but it was more than that. You see, I was afraid.'

Her tension disappeared and she smiled. 'I know. I figured it out.'

'As for my controlling tendencies—'

She placed a finger on his full lips. 'I understand them now, and I'm sorry for jumping to the wrong conclusion. I knew what Walter was like, but it was easier to blame you because of my failure to gain his favor. Forgive me?'

Adam waved the application form she'd completed. 'Only if you'll stay,' he said. 'Be my wife and live in my huge house until we're both too old to practice medicine.'

Naomi couldn't speak; her throat was clogged with emotion. She'd finally heard the words she'd wanted to hear. For a few seconds she collected her thoughts—until his stiff posture and the plea in his eyes registered. She hurried to put him out of his misery.

'I will.' She held out her hand.

He grasped it tightly. 'We don't have much of a career ladder,' he warned.

'Head of Deer Creek's emergency services is a move upward, wouldn't you agree?' She met his gaze.

A smile spread across his face. 'What about the big city, the glamour, the excitement of a huge ER department?'

'What about it?'

'You'll miss it.'

'Yes, but when I visited Lakeside today I found I missed Deer Creek more.' She patted the cushion next to her. 'The Cynthias of this world have those places. I've done my time and I'm ready for other things now.'

He sat beside her. 'I'm glad to hear it because my partnership arrangements don't have escape clauses.'

'Neither do mine.'

He flung his arm around her and pulled her close, before lowering his mouth to hers.

Naomi had only one coherent thought as his touch set her on fire.

She had finally come home.

EPILOGUE

One year later. . .

Adam fastened the hook at the back of Naomi's dress. 'You're all together now,' he said, caressing the spot behind one ear proven to melt her into a puddle.

A familiar and welcome shiver went down her spine. 'If you keep that up I won't be,' she chided without rancor as she rearranged her long tresses. 'We have company downstairs.'

He wiggled his eyebrows. 'They can wait.'

'They can, but this one. . .' she motioned to the crib across the room '. . .can't. I don't want our child to spoil Lacey's and Dale's wedding with a crying spell, not to mention the christening ceremony afterwards. Everything is timed to be over before the next feeding.'

'I suppose.'

She laughed at his crestfallen expression. Throwing her arms around his neck, she planted a swift kiss on his mouth. 'You look like a little boy who's had his favorite toy taken away.'

'I have,' he said solemnly.

'Then I'll make it up to you. Soon.' She hugged him, before stepping back. 'Is everyone here?'

Adam nodded. Holding up his fingers, he counted off their guests. 'Your friends, Beth and Kirsten, are in the kitchen, finding something to settle Kirsty's stomach.'

Naomi smiled, remembering her own bouts with

morning sickness. Unfortunately, Kirsty's seemed to occur all day long.

'Tristan stationed himself at the bannister to keep Jared away from it.' Adam shook his head. 'I've never seen a three-year-old with such a glint in his eye for trouble.'

'Where's Jake?'

'He volunteered to steer Annie away from the flowers, but he hasn't been too successful. Annie doesn't pay too much attention to her uncle Jake so don't look too closely at the flower arrangement on the coffee-table.'

Naomi grinned. Beth had warned of her two-year-old's proclivity before they'd arrived. 'I won't.'

'Mom is helping Lacey and Melissa get dressed. Evelyn and Amy are with Hank, and the rest of the guests are in the garden.' The doorbell rang and Adam glanced at his watch. 'That should be the minister.'

He moved toward the crib and lifted the small bundle. 'It's showtime, little one.'

The baby gave a soft sigh, but didn't awaken.

Naomi mentally went over the list, certain that someone was missing from her husband's recitation. A minute later she knew. 'Dale! What about Dale?'

'The last time I saw him he was with your brother, Mark, pacing the floor in my office.'

Remembering how she'd opened the front door and found her brother on the porch, tall and tanned and handsome in his naval uniform, she smiled. Mark wouldn't admit how he'd managed to get leave right now, and from Adam's Cheshire cat look she was certain he'd been instrumental in arranging it.

Still, she didn't care if Adam had pulled a few strings.

He did it because he knew how much she'd wanted Mark as her child's godfather.

'You're not upset over Hank giving your sister away, are you?'

'Nope.' He looked down at the precious gift in his arms. 'My hands are full. By the way, are you sure about the name for the christening ceremony? It isn't too late to change it.'

Naomi shook her head. 'No. David Alan Parker is perfect. Hank was thrilled by the honor and I can't think of a better way to remember your father. I just hope we made the right decision to combine Lacey's wedding with David's christening ceremony. That's a lot of excitement for a two-month-old.'

'He's going to sleep through most of it, anyway, so don't worry. Besides, with all of the aunts and uncles begging for a chance to hold him, he'll be a happy camper.'

'I hope you don't mind having all the extra people, but I wanted to share this special day with the friends who are like family to me.'

'No problem.' He stroked his son's fine hair. 'You do realize you've given me something I've always wanted.'

'What's that?'

He grinned, his eyes gleaming with merriment. 'An ally in a family of women.'

MILLS & BOON®

Medical Romance

Dear Santa,

Please make this a special Christmas for us.
This Christmas we would like...

A VERY SPECIAL NEED by Caroline Anderson
'Daddy do you think you'll ever find another mummy
for me? I think I'd like to have a mummy,' Alice asked.

A HEALING SEASON by Jessica Matthews
Libby's children loved having Dr Caldwell around at
Christmas, but then it wasn't just the children who
liked him.

MERRY CHRISTMAS, DOCTOR DEAR by Elisabeth Scott
Colin told his Uncle Matt that you couldn't always be
sure what you got for Christmas, you just had to wait
and see, but they felt sure that this Christmas would be
worth waiting for.

A FATHER FOR CHRISTMAS by Meredith Webber
Richard tries hard to put his feelings for Margaret's
children down to a lack of sleep, but he isn't fooling
anybody, not least of all himself!

Christmas is for kids

...a family.
Thank you very much
The Children

Four books written by four authors from around
the world with one wish for Christmas.

Jennifer BLAKE

GARDEN of SCANDAL

She wants her life back...

Branded a murderer, Laurel Bancroft has
been a recluse for years. Now she wants her
life back—but someone in her past will do
anything to ensure the truth stays buried.

*"Blake's style is as steamy as a still July
night...as overwhelmingly hot as Cajun spice."*
—Chicago Tribune

GET TO KNOW
THE BEST OF ENEMIES

the latest blockbuster from TAYLOR SMITH

Who would you trust with your life? Think again.

*Linked to a terrorist bombing, a young student goes
missing. One woman believes in the girl's innocence
and is determined to find her before she is silenced.
Leya Nash has to decide—quickly—who to trust.
The wrong choice could be fatal.*

—

Valid only in the UK & Ireland against purchases made in retail outlets
and not in conjunction with any Reader Service or other offer.

50ᵖ OFF
COUPON

VALID UNTIL: 28.2.1998

TAYLOR SMITH'S *THE BEST OF ENEMIES*

To the Customer: This coupon can be used in part payment for a
copy of Taylor Smith's THE BEST OF ENEMIES. Only one coupon can
be used against each copy purchased. Valid only in the UK & Ireland
against purchases made in retail outlets and not in conjunction with
any Reader Service or other offer. Please do not attempt to redeem
this coupon against any other product as refusal to accept may cause
embarrassment and delay at the checkout.

To the Retailer: Harlequin Mills & Boon will redeem this coupon at
face value provided only that it has been taken in part payment for a
copy of Taylor Smith's THE BEST OF ENEMIES. The company reserves
the right to refuse payment against misredeemed coupons. Please
submit coupons to: Harlequin Mills & Boon Ltd. NCH Dept 730,
Corby, Northants NN17 INN.

9 904170 200509 >

0472 00189